By Ashlee Nix

Content Warnings

- Body Shaming
- Depression
- Self-Harm
- Attempted Sexual Assault
- Past SA Mention
- Murder
- Death
- Toxic/Abusive Family
- No Guaranteed Happy Ending…Yet

Playlist

- Rain by Sleep Token
- Zombie by Yungblud
- Messy by Lola Young
- Falling Away From Me by Korn
- Can You Hold Me by NF feat. Britt Nicole
- Burial Plot by Dayseeker
- Dreamstate by Dayseeker
- Graveyard by Halsey
- Fifteen by Xana (TW SA)
- Dangerous Hands by Austin Giorgio
- Bigger Person by Lauren Spencer Smith
- Are You Really Okay by Sleep Token
- Somewhere Only We Know by Keane
- Die With A Smile by Lady Gaga & Bruno Mars
- Like A Villain by Bad Omens
- The Worst In Me by Bad Omens

For all those who have ever felt like they aren't good enough...
you are

Chapter 1: Olive

New beginnings. That's what this latest move is about. No one in our family has ever owned a house before, so this should be an exciting experience. It would be if anyone wanted me here.

My mother passed away shortly after I was born. Then, when I was six years old, my father, the esteemed history professor Oliver Ambrose, decided he could not handle being my parent anymore and left me with my grandparents. They reluctantly took me in. Most days, I wished they hadn't. My grandmother was indifferent to me on a good day, and my grandfather was nice to me, but didn't seem to care about how my grandmother treated me.

I just graduated from Columbia with my PhD in Archeology and am starting a new job as an Exhibit Developer at the local museum. As long as I can remember, I have wanted to be an archeologist. I saw a newspaper story once on a dig in Egypt. I was drawn in, and that was it. I wanted to know about anything and everything ancient. Maybe that little girl also thought loving history would make her father come back, but that never happened. Now, my dreams of being an archeologist are coming true, and I can finally get away from my family. Before I get started on my own, I am going to stay with my grandparents for a bit longer to save money for my own home.

As I pull up to the grey two story Victorian style house, I am nervous. It's the dread of having to deal with my grandmother again. The house is lovely, honestly nicer than I feel like my grandparents can afford. This is another hair-brained idea Grandmother had gotten Granddad involved in. Her current profession is playing real estate agent; her last failed job was one for those pyramid scheme makeup companies. I do like the house, though. It has a big bay window in the front, a spacious backyard, two giant oak trees in the front, and a large garage addition. I didn't focus on that last part too long. It just felt wrong, off for some reason.

As I am getting out of the car, I hear Grandmother before I see her and her blonde, teased up hair. She calls out, "Finally, there you are! It took you long enough. Now, hurry up and help move these boxes. Good Lord! Did you gain weight, Ollie?"

That woman knows exactly what to say to get to me. Never mind that I have been driving for hours from New York City to Portland, Maine. Then she calls me a nickname I hate and brings up my weight in front of everyone. All the family that is there to help move look my way.

Sighing, I say, "No, Grandmother. I didn't. What do you need me to grab?"

She looks me up and down and finally says, "You know what, just grab your things and get settled. You would probably mess up the flow we have going anyway."

As I walk toward the house, boxes in hand, Granddad greets me. “Hey, Olive,” he says, “your room is upstairs and down the hall, beside the bathroom. I missed you, sweetie.” Yeah, he probably missed the way I took the brunt of Grandmother’s attention.

But I smile, “I missed you too.” He looks like he has aged 10 years since I saw him last summer. That’s what that woman will do to you with her constant nagging and ridicule.

I enter the house, and a heavy, uneasy feeling comes over me. I can’t help but feel like someone is watching me. I brush it off to it being an old, empty space, and maybe one of the cousins had been nearby or something. I head up the stairs to my room to get settled.

I spend the rest of the afternoon bringing my things in and unpacking. My room is nearly finished when Granddad calls me down for dinner. Grandmother bought pizza for everyone. I throw on an oversized sweatshirt, hoping it will make me look smaller and Grandmother won’t make any comments.

I head to the kitchen, grab two slices, and sit down at the table. In front of everyone, Grandmother loudly exclaims, “Oh my, Ollie. Two slices? Are you sure you should eat that? Maybe you shouldn’t eat the pizza at all. Here, I got a salad for you.”

After all these years of her putting me down for being a bit bigger, I've grown used to comments like that. But can anyone ever get used to that? As usual, no one comes to my defense. Instead of making a bigger scene, I accept the salad and eat in silence and sadness.

I finish dinner and head back to my room. Not that anyone notices or cares. I barely get the door closed before the tears flow. I vowed to myself a long time ago to never let my family see me cry. I would get no empathy, only more ridicule. I don't understand what I have ever done to be ostracized from my own family. They all see how Grandmother treats me, and no one says a word. I am worthless in my own family. I don't even have close friends to lean on. I have acquaintances and even the occasional date, but I definitely never bring them home. I don't even know what is wrong with me. Sure, I am a curvy girl and a bit of a loner, but I am compassionate, intelligent, and creative. Yet not one person has ever cared enough to stick around, and if they did, it was out of obligation, not love. In the past, physical pain was my escape from the emotional torment I went through. But while I was away at college, I started going to therapy and learned a few tricks to help through those hard times. I start digging through my boxes and find my journal. Journaling helps to organize my thoughts and feelings when they are just too much for me to cope with.

As I write, I have that feeling someone is watching me again. The same heaviness from earlier is still there, but it also, somehow, feels lighter. As odd as it sounds, it also feels almost curious. I shake my head to clear the thought and the feeling, and continue to write.

My pen quickly moves as I express how I wish that just one person would stand up for me, one person would be there for me, one person would make me feel worth something. I long ago gave up hope that anyone in my family would do that for me. I guess they all look at me and see my mother, the reason my dad left. After she died, apparently, he was never the same, though I never knew any different. I looked like her, and he couldn't stand it. So, he left me with his parents and skipped town. He sent money for my care. He even helped pay for my college, but never had anything else to do with me. I dream of the day I meet someone who will want me for me and not just for sex or as someone to pass the time with. I yearn to be wanted, liked, loved, and accepted for who I am.

I close my journal and put it in the drawer beside my bed. As I go out in the hall to go to the bathroom and shower, I notice the house is quiet. Not that I can hear much since they put me in the room furthest away from everything else. While I really prefer it that way, it still stings that no one wants me here.

After a long, hot shower, I climb into bed and the tears come again. I cry myself to sleep. Welcome home, Olive.

Chapter 2: HIM

New humans are coming into my space today. I loathe being stuck existing here with humans. One would think I would be used to this after hundreds of years of being tied to this land, but I am not. Nor will I ever be. Not to say I am not lonely, because this reality I am living is incredibly lonely. I would just rather be alone than with humans. Today, I am particularly bristly knowing this loud mouthed female with the big hair outside is going to be dwelling in this home. I lose myself in thinking of all the ways I can torture and scare this family away when I hear her shrill voice calling out again. “Where is that girl? She should be here helping! I swear you would think she would be here to help the people she is mooching off of for the next God knows how long!” Great, there is another one coming.

Sometime later, another vehicle pulls into the drive. The other cars and stacked boxes obscure my view, but I am not going outside with that banshee of a woman running around.

Over the years, I have claimed what humans call the “garage” as my domain. I can be quite imposing and tend to make them very uncomfortable when they enter my space. As a result, they do not spend much time there, and I can escape them, even if momentarily. I was once very powerful. Although I must admit I cannot remember much from those times.

My thoughts are again interrupted by these humans. This time, it is by some males in the kitchen area. "I am so glad Olive is finally here now. Grandmother will lay off the rest of us. Come on, let's go get this finished."

Well, I guess it is time for me to go meet the latest intruder. I make my way to the front of the house, spreading a feeling of unease as I do, and I chuckle to myself as I watch these humans squirm. I love to make them squirm. I find my way to the entryway. The older male is speaking to someone as they turn around. Suddenly, all I think is…

HER.

HER.

HER.

That is the only thing I can think of for many moments; it is like the beat of a drum in my head. This must be the one they call Olive. Her wavy, almost snow colored hair frames her gently rounded face. Her eyes are a bright, striking blue, and a few freckles are scattered across her nose like constellations. As I continue to take her in, my attention gets taken by her full, curvy body, and I have a strange and sudden urge to be close to her. She is stunning. Never have I ever seen such a beautiful human. Then she smiled. I would do anything for that smile to be for me. I am shocked at my reaction. Why am I reacting to her like this? I am NOT supposed to like humans. Am I? I cannot seem to remember right now.

By the time I shake from stupor, Olive is already upstairs and headed into her room. I go back to my domain, but my thoughts are all consumed by her.

A short time later, the smell of food drifts in from the kitchen. But even over that, her smell hits me. I go into the kitchen and there she is, the one who has captured my attention. She looks in my direction as if she can see me, but then turns away and heads to where the other humans are sitting. I hear the old one they call "Grandmother" make a comment on what Olive is eating, and, from the look on Olive's face, this has hurt her. As quickly as the hurt came across her face, it leaves and is replaced with a slight smile as she accepts the new meal. No one seems to bat an eye at this interaction, as if it is a regular occurrence. Fury consumes me that someone has slighted Olive. I retreat to my space. As I do, I knock all the food boxes on the floor as I pass. Petty, yes. Effective, also yes. Everyone at the table froze and stared into the kitchen as I entered the garage. What is happening to me? Why am I so protective of a human? Especially one that I have only laid eyes on merely hours ago.

The humans decide there must have been a small earthquake, and that is what pushed their food to the floor. Idiots. They clean up the mess and all leave, except the older male and annoying older female, and, of course, Olive. She does not return from her room after a while, so I go to see what was so important. I enter her room and immediately her tear stained face zeroes in on me as if she can see me, although I know she cannot. No one can. My powers are too weak. All I am good for are parlor tricks now. She shakes her head and looks down at the small book and pen in her lap, and starts writing. As she writes, she gains composure and puts the book away. I slide away from her, although I do not want to, as she passes to go into the hall. She pauses to listen, then sighs and heads to the bathroom. I take my leave and return to the recesses of my space.

Her. A human. She has gained my attention. For all of my existence, I have hated humans. That is one memory I do have intact. Why this one? Why now?

Chapter 3: Olive

I wake up to yelling and cursing from downstairs, so I get up and head down to see what's happening. I reach the bottom of the stairs just in time for Grandmother to scream my name. I turn the corner and see what all the chaos is about. On the wall across from the stone fireplace, in big red letters that look like they are dripping in blood, are the words "GET OUT".

I drop onto the sofa, stunned by the sight. My mind swirls with questions and concerns. Did someone break in during the night? Was this some kind of prank? Could what I have been feeling be the cause of this?

I am pulled from my thoughts when Grandmother grabs my arm, pulling me up. "Why did you do this? I know it was you!"

I stare at her for a second, shocked at the accusation. "No, I didn't! Let go of my arm. You're hurting me!"

She pushes me away, "I know you know something about this."

Granddad walks up, "Come on, Olive. Let's go get some supplies from the garage to clean this up, and then I will go get some paint."

To get to the garage, we have to walk through the kitchen and the attached laundry room. The further back we go, the heavier and darker the feeling is. It feels like something does not want us back here.

I swallow my fear and ask Granddad, "Do you feel that heavy feeling?"

"Oh yes, I believe that there is some wiring that needs to be checked on this side of the house. High EMFs, or Electromagnetic Fields, will often cause those feelings; they can also cause headaches, sleep disturbances, heightened stress levels, worsen mental health symptoms, and even heart trouble if they are high enough," he explains. "I am going to call an electrician out to take a look."

That makes sense. I guess. If it were only on this side of the house, then why did I feel it in my room for a little while last night? No, it was those EMF whatevers, just like Granddad said it was.

We enter the garage, and Granddad starts going through boxes. I ask if I can help, but he mumbles something about knowing where everything is already and just waiting for him. Although for someone who knows where everything is, he sure is looking through a lot of boxes. While I wait, I take in the space. There isn't anything special about it, except that there is a room in the back. I make my way back there, and the closer I get, the higher my anxiety builds until I am practically shaking as I reach the door. It's now or never. I open the door quickly. It immediately feels like I am face to face with someone, yet no one is there. My fear intensifies, but I can't seem to step away. Instead, I put my hand out inside the dark room.

“Olive! I found what I needed. I thought I told you to wait over there for me.” Granddad chastises.

Startled, I stutter, “I…I’m sorry. I was trying to help.” We are about to leave the garage when all of a sudden, the storage room door slams shut.

“It was just the wind," Granddad says. I can only stare at the spot I just stood and notice the clear absence of wind.

I help Granddad clean the paint off the wall, and there is still a faint stain, so Grandmother declares it must be repainted; like a flip of a switch, she is happy and no longer concerned that I had anything to do with this. She states that her “friend” Steve is an excellent painter whom she met through her work in real estate. If she had actually sold one, I might believe her. She calls her “friend” and chats, laughs, and flirts for a while; it is decided that this Steve guy will be painting the living room. If Granddad cares or has concerns, he says nothing. I definitely have my own concerns, considering one of her last male “friends”, Lou, took a liking to a younger me and violated me in ways no one should ever have to go through. Of course, no one believed me. So, the abuse continued until I was too old for him, and he lost interest. I tried to tell someone so many times, and each time I got into trouble for making up stories about such an upstanding person. I got punished so many times that I gave up seeking help and isolated myself. I never wish ill will on anyone who didn’t deserve it. That’s why when he died, I cried tears of joy. He was a monster and absolutely deserved his fate. I would like to think the six years away and therapy have made me stronger. I wish that I didn't have to come back, but it isn't for long, I keep reminding myself. I just need to save a little money to get an apartment. Then, I will be truly free from this family.

To get my mind off everything, I go outside on the deck to lie in one of the loungers and read. Reading is a huge comfort for me. I love so many different genres. This evening, it's a cozy little smut book. Some may think that with my history, it may be triggering to read such material, but I find it empowering to take control and explore my own needs and desires. It has allowed me to take back that piece of myself that was lost all those years ago and heal as much as one can after that kind of trauma. Not everyone views it that way, and that's ok, but it really helps me personally.

I am lying here enjoying the warm summer evening and the beautiful sunset, and I feel someone approaching. I'm tense thinking it is probably Grandmother coming to find something I am doing wrong, but as I turn to see, there's no one there. Correction, someone is definitely there. I just can't see them. I freeze. What should I do? Run? Talk to air? This most certainly is not Granddad's EMFs.

"Okay, well, I am going to shower and go to bed." Talk to air it is. I gather my things and walk quickly back to my room.

Chapter 4: HIM

The old crone screams, and I know she has seen my handiwork. I may not be very powerful these days, but I know how to frighten these puny humans. HA! It will only be a matter of time before they pack back up and move on. They have only been here a few weeks, and I am growing tired of the old woman's attitude, especially towards my…I mean, Olive. The old man is better, but much too passive; there is no fire in him. Olive. Her, I would be almost sad to see go. I have grown quite fond of watching her. I noticed she likes old things; perhaps that is why she keeps the other two humans around. She enjoys reading, writing in her book, and running around outside. I do not see how that is entertaining, but I have noticed many humans enjoy it. Some nights when she comes home from her workplace, she lies outside and watches the stars. I do not go outside much; it reminds me of all that is out of reach for me, but I have ventured out to watch her some nights. Again, my thoughts have strayed to Olive, as they have done for many days since she has been here. I am so deep in thought that I almost miss the reactions to my work. The old man sits in his chair, saying nothing, while that shrill voice echoes in the house. Olive comes from around the corner, her messy waves falling over her shoulders, her ice blue eyes still looking sleepy. Stilled by the sight of her, I barely catch the old woman grab Olive's arm and then push her away. I forget myself for a second and head towards the woman when the old man stands up and asks Olive to come with him. I quickly retreat before I lose all control.

Olive and the old man enter the garage, so I go into the room in the back. It is dark here, but I do not mind. Sometimes in the darkness, clarity reveals itself. Suddenly, I sense someone at the door, and the handle turns.

It is HER.

She is face to face with me but I know she cannot see me. She does not know I am there. Although I can sense her fear, what she does next surprises me. She looks right at me as if she does see me and starts to raise her hand. She is right there in front of me, holding her small hand out. As if my body has a mind of its own, my hand slowly extends to touch hers. We are a whisper away from touching when the old man startles her and she quickly moves away. I slam the door and release the breath I did not realize I was holding.

The sun is setting, and she is lying outside reading again. Although I typically hate being outside of the dwelling, my curiosity wins this day. I slowly walk up behind her. She senses me. She turns around and she freezes. I catch a glimpse at what she is reading and raise an eyebrow. Naughty girl, Olive.

She knows I am here and speaks to me. It does not register what she says, only that she is speaking to me. To me. No one ever speaks to me. Screams, cries, curses, yes, but never speaks directly to me. Her voice is ethereal.

Chapter 5: Olive

I have been working at the museum for about a month now and am enjoying it. Is it exactly what I want to do with my degree? No, but it's a start. My first project is to work with a team to put together a collection of exhibits on local Native American tribes. My project partner is Mark, and he seems nice so far. He is super cute too, with his glasses and short, wavy dark blonde hair. He has the most gorgeous green eyes, a sculpted jawline, and is well over six feet tall. He looks like a model, honestly. We are working so well together tonight that we lose track of time and end up working past closing time. Eventually, we realize we should probably lock up our office and leave for the night.

Since I worked a little late tonight, I changed into my running clothes at work and took a run around the block after I parked at home. I notice someone else's car in the drive, so I begin to mentally prepare myself for whatever I am fixing to face. I walk in the door after my run, and as soon as I am walking by the living room, Grandmother says, “Ollie, come in here and meet my friend, Steve!”

I enter the living room and see Granddad in his chair watching the television in the middle of an utter clusterfuck. Drop clothes, ladders, and painting supplies are strewn about the room, and the walls have been painted; a cream color on top and the brightest red I have ever seen on top of the wainscoting. I feel physically ill. Standing center stage is Grandmother, and who I assume is Steve. Clad in a Hawaiian print shirt and khaki carpenter pants, the thinning blonde man is smiling creepily at me while Grandmother looks at me impatiently.

"Hi Steve, I'm Olive. It's nice to meet you." I say, fighting the rising bile at the way his eyes are roving over my body.

Grandmother must take notice of his interest because she speaks up to say," Oh, Olive, please tell me you didn't go out in public dressed like that! It shows every roll you have!" I know I turn every shade of red. I am so embarrassed.

"I think she looks good," Steve speaks up and gives me a wink.

Grandmother must feel called out because she quickly backslides on her comment, "Oh, I know, I'm just teasing. Ollie, do you like my choice in paints?"

"It's certainly a choice, Grandmother," I say. As I turn to leave, a paint can falls from one of the ladders onto the floor. I mentally thank whoever is responsible for that.

I shower and go to my room for the rest of the evening. I turn on some music and sit down on the bed with my computer and some books to do some research on some of the local tribes we are putting in our exhibit. I am about twenty minutes into my work when I feel someone come into the room. The fear I first felt when we moved in has dissipated, and curiosity has taken its place. I often find myself talking to an empty space when I am alone. Is it really empty, though? Granddad has doubled down on the EMFs but has yet to call an electrician. I think he feels it too, but will never admit it, not to me at least.

"Hi, I promise I'm not doing anything exciting. Actually, I am quite boring, so you will probably get a better show downstairs." I feel the energy move closer until it is like someone is standing next to my bed. A feeling of excitement flows through me, and it both surprises me and doesn't at the same time.

I wait a minute and then say, "Ok, well, watch me work then." I know I literally just invited it to watch me, but it is pretty unnerving having an invisible being watching your every move so closely.

After a few minutes, I settle into a groove, and I can hardly feel anyone there. I do notice when the energy starts moving around the room, looking at all my belongings. I especially notice when the book I have been reading hits the floor. Ok, so that just happened.

"I guess you have seen me reading then. I take it you approve of my choice in reading material?" I say with a chuckle. The book slides towards me. They must really approve. I pick the book up and sit back on the bed. Beside me, the bed dips down and startles me. The air between me and whoever is here is so very charged.

“D…do you want me to read this?” The book opens in front of me. Ok, got it. Read the book. I read for the next ten minutes and thank all that is holy, I didn’t make it to a spicy scene. That would have been really awkward. I begin to yawn, and I feel the book being pushed closed. I take that as a signal they understand I need to sleep. I put the book away, and when I get back in bed, the presence is gone, and I feel so very alone.

Chapter 6: HIM

How is the old man sitting here allowing all of this? His woman is obviously throwing herself at this other male; at this yellow haired male with the facial hair that covers the top of his lip, this male with a shifty gaze. The male returns her attention with a smile, a wink, and light, playful touches. Does he not see this? Does he not care? Although I do not think I would care if that woman were mine. She is despicable. I do not see why he has chosen her as his. Even so, how can he sit there and witness this with such indifference and disinterest? Not that I am protective over this human because he is like every other paltry human I have ever encountered before. I have grown accustomed to watching him tinker in the garage. He has many hobbies, and sometimes Olive will come sit with him. I will admit I do enjoy those times. I shake her from my thoughts and bring myself back into the moment. I watch as the new male and the old hag slather the hideous mix of colors on the walls. I am unhappy that my attempt to scare them did not work, but I am even more disappointed to have been upstaged by her scary tricks with paint.

I go to leave the room, and then I hear Olive walk in. I turn to see her with her platinum hair pulled back, her cheeks pink from her run, and clothes that hug her curves perfectly. I can hardly look away until the old troll upsets her, and then the new male looks at her in a way that makes even my skin crawl. This won't do. I make sure Olive is out of the way, then push the paints over onto the floor, and leave the aftermath to the others.

I sit at the bottom of the stairs, giving Olive time and privacy to shower and change. I do not understand why I am so drawn to her, but I am tired of fighting it, tired of questioning it. I want to see her, watch her, hear her. With that revelation, I am going to try to reveal what I can of myself to her tonight and for once, in my entire existence, hope it does not scare her away.

Once I am sure she is dressed and settled, I enter Olive's room and find her on her bed with books and her computer. She is in a matching top and bottoms covered in pictures of a small cartoon cat with a bow on its head. Her hair, still damp from her shower, is drying in loose curls down her back. I take her in for a few moments. She looks relaxed, a state she is not often in. She says she is boring, and I might find a better show downstairs. I laugh to myself because to me, she is anything but boring. To me, she is interesting, intelligent, caring, passionate, and beautiful. As far as the debacle downstairs, I could not care less about that when given the choice between her and them. With her invitation, I walk over to her and watch her with what appears to be her work, which she has brought home with her. I admire her as she pores over her books and research. Does she not see her passion? Her intelligence? The way she bites her lip as she reads? She is anything but boring. She is…before my thoughts take me further, I look over what she is working on. Things look familiar, but I cannot place them. I am getting flashes of memories, but nothing that explains my past. I keep trying to bring up memories from the back of my mind, but I become frustrated and walk away. I begin looking around her room. I have been in her room many times, but I have never felt the pull to look at her things like I do tonight. Walking around, I see many stuffed fuzzy replicas of animals. A few of them are the cartoon cat on her sleeping clothes. She has small figurines scattered about and different artworks hanging on her walls. I scan her bookcases and spot the book she had been reading the last couple of days lying on one of the shelves. I look at her. If I do what I am about to do, there is no going back. There will be no more doubt; she will know that someone exists here. I take a breath and push the book from the shelf. I could pick it up and bring it to her, but that might be a bit much for first contact, so I stick to simple tactics.

She says I must approve of her choice in reading. While I do enjoy the pink in her cheeks as she reads the more scandalous parts of the texts, I could not care less what they say. I want to watch her in her element: the way she bites her lip, when she tucks her hair behind her ear. I fear I have become hopelessly, utterly obsessed with her. I push the book closer. She picks it up. I sit on the bed beside her, leaning against the back of the bed with my legs stretched out before me. I am so close to her. The urge to touch her is overwhelming, but I do not. I want her to know me before I make any physical contact. After her reaction to the male downstairs, I sense something bad has happened to her in the past, and I do not wish to make her uncomfortable with my touch. The air between us is thick with the feeling of excitement. I open the book, hoping she will take the cue and read aloud, which she does. I listen to her angelic voice read the text to me. After some time, she begins to yawn, and I know it would be selfish to keep her up longer. I push the book, signaling her to close it, and when she gets up to put the book away, I get off the bed and take a last look at her and leave for the night. I go to the room next to hers instead of my space so I can stay close. Still, I have never felt so alone.

Chapter 7: Olive

Ever since that night, what I have been calling the spirit has visited me. Sometimes it watches me work, and other times I will read while it sits on the bed. A couple of nights, I chatted away about work and life while doing my nails. I must be crazy not to be scared of a ghost and actually befriend it. Maybe I should research ways to communicate with spirits and try to find a way for us to actually be able to talk. It can obviously manipulate objects, so maybe that could be a starting point. Yep, definitely crazy.

It's the weekend, so I have slept in a bit later. Maybe Grandmother is out busy with her latest career change. Interior design. Steve convinced her that she had real talent and should work with him at his construction business to provide an extra level of service. So far, no takers, so she has been doing clerical work. She has been in a good mood, though, so she has laid off of me some. Win-win, I guess. Steve has been hanging around more, so that's a loss for me because he is increasingly creepy with each visit. He hasn't done anything really inappropriate. Grandmother is even on her best behavior around him, not insulting me so much. It's the way he looks at me when he thinks I am not paying attention. It's the vibe he gives off. Maybe I am just seeing things where there is nothing. I mean, hell, I am kind of friends with a ghost. So perhaps I am not the best at judging these things.

I go downstairs to the kitchen to make a little breakfast. Grandmother is in the kitchen when I get there, making something on the stove.

"Let me know when you're finished, and I will make myself something," I say.

"Do you want me to make you some of what I am making your Granddad, Ollie?" she replies.

I hate that nickname, and she knows it, but against my better judgment, I accept her momentary and rare kindness. Whatever she is making smells odd, but I keep that to myself in order to keep the peace this morning. I go to the fridge and get out the orange juice. I spill some on the counter when I pour it, so I grab a paper towel and clean it up. When I go to throw it away, I notice a can of dog food in the garbage. We don't have a dog.

"So, Grandmother, what are you cooking?" I question, clearly now knowing the answer.

"Oh, just a new recipe I found for beef and gravy," she has the audacity to reply.

"Grandmother! I saw the dog food can in the garbage! You were going to feed us DOG FOOD!" I yell. A heaviness fills the kitchen, and I know precisely what is present at this point. She shakes the feeling off, her only tell that she feels it too.

"Oh, Ollie, it was just a harmless prank. It is funny," she coldly replies.

"*What is wrong with you?* That is not funny at all!" I feel the sting of the slap before I know what is happening.

"How dare you speak to me that way, you ungrateful cow. You should be kissing my feet and eating anything that I think you deserve. I took you in and raised you. I should have made your father give you to any orphanage that would take an ugly creature like you," she spits with disdain. A dark, rage filled feeling came over the room, and before Grandmother could continue her hate filled rant, every pot and pan from the cabinets came across the room at her. None of them actually hit her, but her eyes went wide, and a wet spot appeared on the front of her pants. If I weren't in a bit of a shock at all that had just transpired, I would have laughed. She stared at me for a minute and then ran off A moment later, I heard her bedroom door slam. She avoided me the rest of the day.

"Thank you, whoever you are. That was brilliant! I have never seen her so unraveled," I spoke to my ghost. I pick up the mess and dump Grandmother's meal into the trash and head back to my room. My appetite is ruined for the morning.

I am sitting in my bed, and my phone goes off. My phone never goes off unless it's work, or sometimes my old college roommate checks in on me. She is the only one I have ever confided in about my family. I grab my phone, and it is Mark from work. Maybe he wants to go in and do some extra work on the exhibit. We are ahead of schedule because we work so well together, so that can't be it. Oh no, what if something happened at the museum? I quickly open the message. I am relieved that there is nothing bad, but I am very nervous about what he has asked. He and a few of our coworkers are going out for drinks and trivia night at a bar in the next town over, and would like me to join. No one ever asks me to join. What should I do? How do I act? What do I wear? After the morning, I had a night out might be nice. I tell him that I would love to go and would meet them there. He sends the location and time they are meeting. I hit the shower and get ready.

On my drive there, an intrusive thought breaks through. What if they are setting me up, and I get to the bar and no one is there, and this was all just a cruel joke? My thoughts drift back to a time in middle school when a group of kids, who I thought were my friends, and who swore they were, voted for me to be most likely to join a popular weight loss program. Of course, that was not an official school vote but just a poll that the students in my grade had for various things. They said it was a joke, just for fun. It didn't feel very fun to me, though. It felt like a knife through my heart at the time. No, no, I have worked with Mark for a couple of months now, and he really doesn't seem like the type that would do such a thing. Olive, get it together! I am a perfectly nice person and deserve to make friends and have a good time.

I pull into the parking deck for "The Loft", a huge bar and entertainment center built in an old factory. I check my makeup, adjust my clothes, and take a deep breath. I got this. As promised, Mark and a few of our coworkers were standing outside the entrance waiting for me. So far, so good.

"There she is! Hi Olive, we were all so happy you could make it!" Mark exclaimed.

"OMG! I love your top! That is your color, girl! You look beautiful!" a girl named Candy said. I recognized her from one of the other teams at the museum. I'm about 5'9" and she is a few inches shorter than me, with dark blonde hair and bright green eyes. Her teammate Jennifer is here too. I recognize her because I have always loved her chin length dark brown bob.

"Thank you! I am so glad you guys invited me. I am definitely overdue for a night out." I say. With that, we go inside and find a table. Apparently, at trivia night, you need group names. After a hilarious debate, we decide on "The Brainy Bunch," and much to our delight, the theme of the night is historic figures. Of course, we nail it and win. We stay until midnight and then say our goodbyes. Mark walks me to my car, and we wish each other a good weekend and part ways.

I get home around 1:00 in the morning and quietly enter the house. As I pass the living room, Granddad is sitting in his chair, and I feel my ghost friend in the room as well.

"Olive, is everything okay? Your grandmother told me what happened this morning. You shouldn't have blown up like that; it only antagonizes her," Granddad says.

“ME! She was going to feed us dog food! She said vile things to me!” I whisper yell.

“She said it was just a joke and she would not have let us eat it. You didn’t need to throw anything at her either,” he rebutted. Ah, so she blamed it on me! Thanks, ghost friend, for trying to help, but apparently even a ghost can’t do anything right. The lights flicker rapidly.

“I really need to call that electrician. Anyway, just try to steer clear of her until this blows over, sweetie. For all of our sake.”

Well, so much for my good mood. How can he take her side? Why can’t he see what kind of person she is? No. No, they will not ruin my night. I made new friends and had a fantastic night. I go upstairs, brush my teeth, wash my face, brush out my hair, and change into a tank top and shorts. As I enter my bedroom, I feel someone enter behind me, and the door closes quietly behind us. I turn around as if something has changed, and I would be able to see someone, but still nothing. Something is there, though, I can feel them. They are close. So, close I think I could touch them if I put out my hand. I lift my hand as if to touch someone’s face. My hand touches something warm, like someone leaning into my touch. Something is definitely there. I slowly remove my hand, turn, and go to bed. I should say something. Say something, Olive.

“Goodnight.” Smooth, Olive. I turn out the light and turn to go to sleep. I feel them still standing in the spot

I left them. As I drift off, I can't help but think something has changed tonight. Something big.

Chapter 8: HIM

For the past weeks, I have spent more time with Olive. Just sitting with her while she works, she tells me about her day. Sometimes she paints her fingernails and toenails in delicate colors. She still reads to me, even though it is never anything scandalous like she reads to herself. I wish she would. I would love to see her cheeks in that pretty shade of pink they turn when she is aroused, but self conscious about it.

I never knew what I was missing out on by not befriending a human. Although none of them would be Olive. She is one of a kind. Olive is fearless. She does not cower in my presence or fear me. She accepts me and is trying to learn about me and how to communicate with me. No. No other human would do, only her. Although I do not believe I am what she calls a ghost, maybe the same methods will work.

Olive heads downstairs where the old witch is in the kitchen, standing over some putrid brewing on the stove. The woman has been in better moods recently. I attribute this to the other male. I do not like this male, though. He looks at Olive too long and too often. At least the woman has not bothered Olive recently. I go to the garage with the older male, who is fiddling, as he calls it, with some machine. He is a quiet male and keeps to himself, and is often out here working on projects.

I hear Olive yelling in the kitchen, and I rush in to see what is wrong. It seems the brew was food meant for dogs, and she was going to feed it to Olive. She is disgusting. When I see the slap, I am sent over the edge, and there is no going back. The venom that is spewed next is sickening. How could someone speak such things to someone so gentle as Olive? I summon all the power I can and slam the cabinet doors open and throw any and every object in them at the hag. I laugh as she pisses herself and runs away.

I do not like watching Olive clean up my mess, but I am afraid it will scare her if I do it. So, I stand watch and make sure that old hag does not come back. Olive gets finished and makes her way back to her room. I follow her to make sure she is okay. She sits on her bed with her computer and starts her research on how to communicate with me again. Her portable phone goes off. In the months she has been here, it rarely goes off. I look over her shoulder, and it is someone named Mark. Is Mark a male's name? I do not like this. I do not like this at all. I leave the room before I see more. Before I know it, she is coming down the stairs looking like a vision in her emerald green top and jeans that hug her perfectly. Her curls are more defined than usual, and she is wearing more makeup than she usually does. No. No, I do not like this at all.

Why am I so concerned, so possessive? It is not as if she is mine. She does not even know I exist. That revelation hurts more than I thought it would. I used to pride myself on my coldness and ability not to be attached to these disgusting little humans. Until her. She is the remedy to a sickness I did not know I had. She is the light to my darkness. She is a spiritual awakening I did not know I needed.

While I was lost in thought, she left. I turn just in time to see her car leave the driveway. The old man is in the living room watching television, so I sit on the couch and let all thoughts leave my head for a little while. I must admit I see the appeal in television. He is currently watching something on the origins of these lands. Things start looking familiar, really familiar. The red coats, the native symbols. My mind is swirling with information, trying to make sense of it. Before I can make any headway, the television clicks off, and there stands the ogress herself.

She stands before the old man in his chair and recounts the events of the morning. All complete lies, of course. When he does not say much, she screeches at him about how he needs to have her back, and he has to live with her after Olive is gone, so he better do something about this. She stomps back off to her lair. The old man lets out a breath and turns the television back on.

It is several hours later when Olive quietly comes in. I make myself known so she will know I am here. The old man calls her over and comments on what that lying woman told him. To no surprise, he takes her side. Olive defends herself, but he continues his stance. I flicker the lights with irritation. He says something about calling someone out for the lights and asks Olive to essentially keep the peace, as if that is her responsibility. She turns and goes upstairs.

When she emerges from the bathroom, she is in the least amount of clothes I have ever seen her in. I am in awe. Her creamy skin is so smooth, I ache to reach out and touch her. As she goes into her room, I follow and close the door behind me. I turn around, and she is facing me as if she is trying to see me. I wish she could see me. She reaches her petite hand up towards my face. I lean into it and close my eyes. Her touch is warm, and her hand is as soft as I thought it would be. I want that hand to explore more, but instead, she slowly lowers it. She turns, climbs into bed, and softly whispers, "Goodnight". Leaving me standing there, knowing something has changed and there is no going back.

Chapter 9: Olive

Work this week has been great! I have gone out to lunch with Mark a couple of times, and one day, we joined some of the other teams. Since it is Friday, the group has decided to go out again tonight to an adult arcade. It sounds like so much fun. I can't wait! It feels like everything is finally falling into place for me. I have been saving money, and hopefully I will be able to move to my own place and away from my family sometime after the holidays.

I have also doubled down on my efforts to find a way to communicate with my ghost. I read about these things called EVPs, Electronic Voice Phenomenon. You have a recorder recording as you ask questions, and then you play it back, hoping to hear the voice of a spirit answering you. This afternoon, I bought a small digital voice recorder to try to talk to my ghost. After I get home tonight, I plan on trying it out.

I have effectively avoided Grandmother this week, but as I pull in after work, I notice Steve is here. That means she is here too. Deep breath, Olive, you can do this. All I need to do is get upstairs, get ready, and leave again for our group night. I enter as quietly as I can. I think I am in the clear until I hear "Ollie! You're home!" Great. Let's get this over with.

I walk into the dining room where the table is littered with different paint, flooring, and fabric samples. Standing proudly in front of them is Grandmother, and beside her is Steve. Granddad is nowhere around, so I assume he is tinkering in the garage. I also feel the absence of my friend, which is odd because I normally feel them as soon as I open the door.

"Ollie, I got my first designing job. Isn't that wonderful?" she asks.

"Yes, Grandmother, that is quite the accomplishment. Congratulations." I stand there awkwardly for a second under Steve's stare and Grandmother's oblivious, giddy grin and then add, "Well, I'd better go. I am meeting some friends in a bit. I will be out a little later, so don't worry."

"I wouldn't worry, Ollie. That's good, you *finally* have some friends. You're so odd, I thought it would never happen," she says, chuckling.

Steve chimes in, "I don't think she's odd. I think Olive is a *fine* young woman." The way he said it and the way he eyed me made my skin crawl, but I thanked him and quickly left the room.

I finally get upstairs to get ready, and still no sign of my friend. This is really strange, but I really need to get going. So, I touch up my makeup and do my hair. I pick out a royal blue sweater that hangs off one shoulder, showing just the right amount of skin, and a pair of fitted jeans, a perfect outfit for a cool September night. I am definitely feeling myself tonight. As I head down the stairs, I feel my friend at the bottom of the staircase.

“I was a little worried you forgot about me,” I whispered, “I have a surprise for you tonight! I will be back later.” As I walk out the door, I check myself in the mirror, and I swear I hear a low growl.

I am having such an incredible time at the arcade! I am so glad I have found this group of people. I really feel like I have found my tribe. We have so much fun on the old school games, cheering each other on as we try to beat each other's high scores. We bowl and are all very competitive and quite serious about our forms. Laser tag is a blast. I am doing great until my clumsiness shows, and I trip over my own feet. Mark is there to catch me before I can hit the ground. We are laughing, and I apologize for being so clumsy, and I said, “I hope I didn’t hurt you. I know I am heavy.”

He replied, “You aren’t heavy at all, Olive. What guy wouldn’t want a beautiful woman in his arms?” We both chuckle and continue on with trying to tag all our friends.

I pull into the driveway, and all the lights are off. Steve’s car is gone. Phew. I enter the house as quietly as I can and immediately feel a presence at the bottom of the steps.

“Did you sit and wait on me?” I ask. It moves, and I head up the stairs to the bedroom. Grabbing a nightgown, I head to the bathroom to change and wash up. When I go back to my room, my friend is waiting for me.

"Someone is ready for their surprise," I chuckle as I pull out the recorder. "This should be able to record your voice. I will ask a question, and you can answer or say whatever you want right here in this red light. When I play it back, I should, hopefully, be able to hear what you said," I explain, "Let's do this, my friend!"

"Let's start simple and say hello," I wait a few seconds, and then play the recording back, and I was not ready for what it says.

A VERY clear, "Well, hello, love," comes through. The voice is definitely male, deep, thick, and powerful; warmth spreads directly to my core. What the hell is wrong with me? A ghost voice, really? A really, really, seductive ghost voice, but still. Okay. Get it together, Olive.

"What is your name?" I ask.

"I do not know." There is a hint of an accent there, but I can't quite place it.

"Where are you from?"

"I do not know."

Hmm…okay, maybe something more recent.

"Where were you early tonight before I left?"

"With the old man."

"Oh, I see, ditching me for a new friend," I say with a laugh.

"Not my friend. You are my friend."

Well, that gives me all the warm fuzzies. He is a loyal ghost.

"Do you know that you are a ghost?"

"Not a ghost."

"Well, I can't see you. That must mean you're a ghost, right?"

"Not a ghost. I am alive. I am trapped."

Alive? Trapped? Is that possible? How is that possible?

"How are you trapped? How do I free you?"

I yawn.

"Olive, you need sleep. We will talk later."

"No. No! I want to help you! Please tell me!"

"Goodnight, my Olive." My Olive? For some reason, that is comforting and honestly kind of sexy. Seriously, Olive. Get it together!

"Will you stay with me for a while?"

"Yes."

I settle into bed, my mind reeling. He is a ghost, right? He has to be. I mean, I can't see him or hear him. Would he know if he was dead? What if he is something else? The recordings were clearer than anything I heard on the internet. What if he is trapped? Should I help him? Can I help him? Is he good? Is he evil? These thoughts run through my head as I drift off to sleep.

Chapter 10: HIM

How did I miss her coming home? I quickly walk through the house, noting the troll and her weird male in the dining room. As I walk by, I send papers flying through the air and laugh as the male exclaims, "What the hell?". I catch sight of her coming down the stairs. She is divine. Her cascading, silky hair frames her delicate features, and the royal color of her clothing only brings out her piercing blue eyes.

She says she has a surprise for me when she gets back. Where is she going? Who is she going to be with? Will it be this Mark male who messaged her recently? I do not like this. No, not at all. Before I realize it, I let out a growl. She turns as if she heard me. Interesting.

I wait by the stairs for a while, but then decide I am not some smitten fool and will not wait for her return like this. I go to find the old man. To no surprise, he is in his chair watching the television. Tonight's show is about treasure hunting. I sit with him for a couple of hours and then move back to the stairs. Perhaps, I am a smitten fool after all.

The door opens and Olive quietly walks in, bathed in moonlight. Yes, quite the smitten fool. She senses me immediately and asks if I was waiting for her. I have been caught. We head up the stairs, and I wait in her room for her. She comes in wearing a short dressing gown, and I have to avert my gaze from her bare legs before I get lost in thought. She asks if I am eager for my surprise, and I must admit, I have actually forgotten about it. She pulls out this small device and explains how to speak into it and how it is supposed to work. I speak into it. For a moment, I am afraid I was too forward, but by the pink in her cheeks and the smile on her face, my words had their intended effect.

She asks me a series of questions that should be easy, but I do not know the answers. As always, there is some kind of block to my past. She asks if I am a ghost. Of course, she would think that, but I am no ghost. I am a being. A living, breathing being. I am trapped, as if by some kind of curse. I would have gone into more detail, but she begins to yawn, and I know that she is exhausted from her various activities today. So, I say goodnight. Then, she asks me to stay. How can I deny that request?

She settles into bed, rolling over to face me. I want to reach out my hand and stroke her smooth cheek, touch her soft hair, but I deny myself. I have had far longer to want her. She does not know me yet. She will, though. I know for certain. I want her to know me.

Chapter 11: Olive

I wake up still thinking of last night. As I lie in bed, all I can think about is the sound of his voice and the way he said I was his. I find that oddly comforting. Something stirs beside me. It is him. He stayed, just as he said he would. I turn and smile. There is a lightness about him, and I know that he is smiling too. I wish I could know what he looks like. I grab the recorder.

"Thank you for staying with me. I'm sure you were bored."

"I will stay whenever you ask it of me. I slept. I was not bored."

"Oh. I didn't realize you slept."

"I am not a ghost, Olive", he sounds amused.

I giggle and get up, accidentally flashing him my panties. I quickly pull down my gown. Oops. I hope he isn't a shy…whatever he is. I grab some clothes and let him know I am going to get dressed. The last thing I want is to go downstairs and run into Steve. To have to endure his stares at my bare legs sounds like the worst way to begin any day.

I walk through the living room with my friend following me. We find Grandmother and Granddad both watching television, which is a bizarre sight, but whatever. "Good morning," I say to both of them as I walk through. I don't get a response from either. Fine by me. It's better than the alternative of having Grandmother insult me. My friend isn't here with me now. I guess he figured I didn't need him for this part. I really need a better name for him other than, well, him. I make an egg and cut up some berries. I grab a container of yogurt and a bottle of water, and as I head out of the kitchen, I run right into Grandmother. My plate goes all over her and the floor. A sneer comes across her face.

"You are a stupid waste of space. What the hell do you think you are doing coming around the corner like that? Well, that gut of yours came around before you did, didn't it? You're so disgusting. I can barely look at you anymore. If you get any bigger, you are going to be as big as the fat lady in the freak show at the circus!" She flipped her hair, laughed, and walked away casually. She turned back to say, "I see how you look at Steve. Just like you used to look at Lou, don't bother. He nor anyone else could ever want something as hideous as you, Ollie." I am left standing there, dumbfounded at what just happened, eyes full of tears.

I leave the mess on the floor and numbly walk back to my room. Granddad is sitting in his chair, so close to where we were. I know he heard every single word. Yet, he says nothing as I walk by. He just keeps watching television. I do notice the volume is louder. Does he agree? He definitely doesn't defend me. How could someone who is supposed to love me always be so cruel? I don't understand. I will never be good enough. I don't know who to be. Maybe she's right. Maybe I am not good enough. Maybe I am a waste of space. A hideous, freak.

I go into my room and lock the door. I can't stop the tears now. I am sobbing at this point. What did I ever do to her? Why me? Why am I not enough? I am not enough. I am not enough for her, for my family. I am not enough for my father. I am not enough for anyone. I can hardly see through the tears as I search through my drawer and find my marker. Another therapy strategy for when things are too much. Take a marker and mark on my arm instead of cutting it. I mark on my arm. Slash. Slash. Slash. It's not enough. It's not enough. IT'S. NOT. ENOUGH. I'm panicking. I can't catch my breath. I see a box cutter, and before I know it, it's in my hands. I am on autopilot at this point. I don't even get the first cut in, and the cutter is flying across the room, and I am pulled into his arms. I didn't even feel him come in. He feels so strong and warm. The earthy scents of vetiver and fallen rain invade my senses. He doesn't let go, and I don't pull away. I just lean in and cry.

After a while, I pull away, and while he seems reluctant to let me go, eventually he does. I pick up the recorder.

"Can you lie here and hold me?"

"Anything you need, my Olive."

We climb into bed, and I feel his strong arms come around me and pull me close. As I doze off, I swear I feel a breath on my neck.

Chapter 12: HIM

She rolls over and smiles. I want all of her smiles like this every day. She is perfect. I know she cannot see me, but I smile back. When was the last time I smiled? I do not remember. Definitely not in this place. She gets up, and I see a flash of her underwear and part of her bottom. I am glad she cannot see me right now. She pulls down her gown and gives me a cheeky grin. Naughty girl, Olive.

I follow her downstairs. She speaks to the others, but they do not talk back, which is odd because the old hag always has something to say. I glance at the television and realize it is another show that has objects I recognize. Again, red coats, symbols, artifacts, and the male speaking says something about French soldiers. All of this is so familiar but just out of reach for me. I glance over, looking for Olive, and I find her tearful and heartbroken, her breakfast on the floor. In front of her, the evil bitch herself spews nasty, vicious lies to my sweet Olive. I go over, but Olive, as if oblivious to me, walks past.

I give her a little time to herself after that. How could someone hate her so much? She is the purest soul I have ever met. She is so beautiful and gentle. It has to be jealousy and spite. Even that does not excuse it. I quickly clean up the leftover mess before the others can see and head towards Olive's room. I need to check on her. I will deal with the bitch later.

She has locked the door. That is unlike her. She always leaves it unlocked for me. I can go through it, but I do not like to. I do not want to invade her privacy. I lean on the door to see if I can hear her, to make sure she is okay. I listen to her crying, and she sounds frantic. I know I probably should not, but I feel the need to check on her. I go through the door.

Terror courses through me when I see her on the floor with blood all over her arms. No, not blood. It is drawings. I release a breath. She grabs a sharp box cutter, and it registers with me what she intends to do with it. I rush to her side and slap it from her hands. She looks at it and then turns towards me with her tear stained face. She stands, and I grab her and pull her close. I will not lose my Olive this day.

She eventually calms, but I continue to hold her. I cannot let her go. She pulls back and gets her recorder. She asks if I will hold her, and I say I will. I would do anything she asks of me. At this point, I am completely and utterly hers. We climb into bed, and I pull her close and hold her as she falls asleep. Her scent is intoxicating, like lavender and vanilla.

I watch her sleep for a while and notice her hair has fallen in her face. I tuck it behind her ear and start to doze myself. I fall asleep with my hand resting lightly on her head in her hair.

Chapter 13: HIM

I woke expecting Olive to be beside me. Instead, I find her side of the bed empty. I quickly sit up and look around frantically, afraid of what I might find. I see her standing at the end of the bed, staring with wide eyes directly at me.

"Who are you? How did you get here?" she questions.

"You can see me?"

"Of course, I can see you! You're in my bed!"

"Olive, it is me."

"Who are you?"

"I do not know, my Olive."

"Oh my God. You're HIM. I mean, you. I mean, the not-ghost," she stammers.

"Yes, it is me. I am sorry, I do not remember my name."

She gets on the bed and slides close to me. She puts her hand on my face and looks into my eyes. For several moments, we just look at each other.

"You are beautiful," she blurts.

"Olive, you are the most stunning creation that ever was," I say as I slide my hand to her cheek.

She goes to say something else, but her concentration is broken, and she looks down at her arm. I look down as well. All of her markings are gone. We went to sleep, and she still had them on her. We look at each other, coming to the same conclusion. We haven't woken up yet. We are able to see each other in a dreamstate.

"How is this possible?" she wonders aloud.

"I am not sure. I do have power. Maybe this is one of them? I have never wanted to know a human before, so I do not know."

"So, you're not human? What are you?"

"I do not know. I am living, but trapped."

"Like a curse?"

"Yes, perhaps. I do not remember much, my Olive."

"Why do you call me that?"

"Because you are mine."

"Oh, really. Don't I get a say in this?" she chuckles.

"Of course you do. I would never take your choices from you. But know I am yours. I have been yours since I laid eyes on you, Olive."

“Why are you so interested in me? I mean, you're gorgeous. Like, seriously, god-like, and I am, well, this,” she gestures to me and then herself.

“Olive, how do you not see what I see? You are intelligent, caring, strong, passionate, and incredibly beautiful. Olive, you're the most beautiful woman I have ever seen. I have been around for many, many years, and no one has even come close to catching my attention as you have. From the first time I saw you, something stirred inside my soul, and I knew then that my heart already had begun its journey to yours.” Her eyes fill with tears, and she averts her gaze.

“How long have you been here?” she quietly changes the subject. She is not in the same place that I am in, and that is okay, but she needs to know she has changed me, and she is worth everything to me.

“I do not know exactly, but hundreds of years at least.”

“Are you trapped in this house?”

“No, I can leave this place, but I am tied to the land that it sits on. I do not like to go outside. It reminds me of all that I cannot remember and all that I am missing.”

“I have felt you outside with me before, or are there others here?”

“There are no others here. I have only gone outside to be with you,” I say quietly.

"Olive, can we talk about earlier? Only if you would like to. I will not push you."

"It is okay. I had a momentary relapse. I thought I was past letting Grandmother hurt me, but I guess not. I typically write in my journal, go for a run, or, when it is really awful, use my markers. I panicked really badly and lost control. That usually doesn't happen."

"I have seen you do these other things and wondered what they were for. Thank you for explaining them to me. Olive, know that this beast of a woman is wrong and all the vicious venom she spews is just that, and there is no truth in it."

"Thank you," she says quietly.

Suddenly, there is a feeling like we are being pulled away from each other, and there is a panicked look on her face. Without thinking, I grab her hand, "I think one of us is waking up. So do not worry, Olive. Anytime you sleep, I will be here with you until you tell me to go." Her smile is the last thing I see before I open my eyes to a dark room.

Chapter 14: Olive

I open my eyes, and the room is already dark. My phone says it's 8:00 p.m. I have slept all day. WOW. What a dream. I have never had such a vivid dream before. Was that dream real? It couldn't have been. Could it? As if in answer to my questions, someone shifts beside me. I know who is beside me without even turning, but I grab the recorder and roll over. I feel him facing me.

"Was that dream real?" I ask.

"Yes, I remember it too."

I wish I could see him now. He is so damn gorgeous. He is indigenous and a warrior, as evidenced by the bands of leather, beads, and bone I saw circling his arms. He wore a short sleeved tunic that was untied, revealing his very toned and muscular abs, and some type of animal hide pants. He has to be close to 7' tall. Almost seven feet of solid muscle, and tattooed muscle at that. His long, midnight black hair flows down to his mid back, and oh, how I could get lost in his onyx eyes, so dark and endless. Olive, snap out of it, woman!

I lie there a few more minutes before I feel a caress on my face and my hair tucked behind my ear. I smile and say, "I am going to shower and wash all of the marker away. Will you be here when I get back?"

"Yes, my Olive. I will stay," he replied.

I get in the shower and let the water run over me as I try to process the day I have had. I can't believe that I lost myself like that over Grandmother. I should be used to her by now. No. What she does is wrong, and I shouldn't have to be used to it. I shouldn't feel bad for backsliding earlier, either. This is a process. I just need to stick to my methods and keep on trying my best.

My thoughts drift to HIM. We really need to figure out his name. Why is he so enamored with me? I am nothing special, but the way he said my name like a prayer and the heat in his eyes when he looked at me, I felt like I was. Just the thought of him warms me straight in my core. By mid shower, I have myself so worked up thinking about his strong hands all over me that I am in desperate need of release. I slowly move my hand to the V between my legs and dip two fingers inside of my wet heat, and then begin circling my clit with slow, deliberate pressure. I imagine it is him pleasuring me as the pressure continues to build until pleasure floods my senses. I let out a moan before I can stop it. As I come down, all I can think is I really hope he didn't hear that.

I come back to my room, entering almost shyly. I'm sure my face will give me away. Then I notice that all the mess from earlier has been cleaned up. As promised, he is still there. I pick up the recorder.

"Thank you for cleaning up. I have been thinking, and maybe I could do some research and figure out who you are and how to free you. How does that sound?"

“I would like that, Olive.” He said quietly, and then I felt his hand on mine.

“I’m going to turn on the recorder, and I want you to tell me a few things from before. Anything you can remember, okay. Then, I will play it back and start researching things. Maybe we can find something useful for you. Go.”

“The old man was watching a show with red coated soldiers and also these symbols and relics that were very familiar but that I could not place. I do know I was very powerful. That is all I can remember for now, Olive. I am sorry.”

“Don't apologize! That is a great start!” I smile encouragingly. “I will grab my computer, and we can get started. I can’t promise miracles, but I can promise to try my best.” I grab my laptop and settle on the bed. I feel the spot next to me dip and a warm presence next to me. Even without seeing him, I feel something in my core just knowing he is close. Refocusing my mind, I search up red coats to make sure that he is, in fact, speaking of British soldiers. There are undoubtedly several times when the British and indigenous people in America overlap in history. Still, the most notable are during the setting up of colonies, the French and Indian War, and the Revolutionary War. So hopefully this will narrow things down a bit and possibly jog some more memories.

“Are these the red coats that you remember?”

“Yes. Are you sure you want to do this tonight?” His care for my well-being is comforting, and I know it's genuine.

“Yes, it will help keep my mind busy. Thank you for being concerned, though. I really do appreciate it. Look! We have our first clue to finding out your past!”

Before I can start another search, there is a soft knock at my door. I get up to open it, and he puts himself between me and the door protectively and slowly opens it. Granddad is standing on the other side holding a plate with a sandwich, chips, and a bottle of water.

“I haven’t seen you since this morning and thought you might be hungry,” he says quietly, handing me the plate and bottle.

“Thank you, Granddad.” With that, he walks down the hall and down the stairs. There's so much hanging in the air, so much unsaid, so much I want to say but can’t. I think I am afraid of the answers to my questions. If I don’t ask them, there is still the possibility of love there. Of redemption.

I set the food down on the bedside table, pick up my computer, and grab the recorder. I get set up on the bed and get ready to begin the search again.

“Okay, are you ready to continue?”

“No. You need to eat my Olive.”

"I will be fine a little longer. According to Grandmother, it wouldn't hurt for me to skip a couple of days of eating." Ouch, too soon. I just hurt my own feelings.

"Olive, do not listen to the rantings of the bitch. You are simply perfection. Eat."

"Okay, bossy," I say with a chuckle. His words warm me, though. Never have I been spoken to this way. I could definitely get used to it.

I grab the plate and realize it's my favorite sandwich, cajun ham with mayo, mustard, lettuce, and tomato. There is only one store that sells this meat, and I didn't buy it. How did he know? What does this mean? Does he actually care about me? Why not stand up for me? I swallow the questions down with my sandwich. Even if I asked them, I would never get the love I so desperately want from my family. My phone dings, bringing me out of my thoughts. It's Mark wanting to know if I'm up for a drag brunch tomorrow. I message him back, letting him know that I am absolutely in. Oh, I can't wait. This is exactly what I need after today. Well, that and maybe another dream visit from a certain hunky guy. Seriously, Olive, get it together, woman! As if summoned, I feel the bed dip beside me.

"Are you ready to get back to our research?"

"Not tonight. I want more dreams with you."

“Surprisingly, I am still tired even after sleeping so much today. I will go brush my teeth, and I will be back.”

I come back into the room and climb into bed. Immediately, I am pulled into his waiting arms and am surrounded by his scent. I feel his hands in my hair, and it doesn’t take long until I fall asleep.

Chapter 15: Olive

I turn over and am drawn into the gravity of his onyx eyes. His bronze, muscular arm is still draped over my waist. He smiles, and I just know I am smiling back like a giddy idiot. I can't help it. The man, or whatever he is, is the most gorgeous thing I have ever seen. I wish he could be like this in the waking world. Then again, he probably wouldn't even look twice at me in the waking world. Just like that, I am snapped out of my stupor like I poured a bucket of ice water on myself.

"What is wrong, my Olive?"

"Just thinking about how if you were able to be free in the waking world, you would have no interest in me," I blurt out. Wow, dream me has no filter.

"Of course I would. You are mine, Olive. Whether we are awake or asleep, you are meant for me. I know this." He almost sounds offended, so I drop it.

I sit up and grab a notebook and a pencil. "Do you think you can draw the symbols that looked familiar to you? I know they won't be here when we wake, but if I can remember them, then I can research them for you." He sits up in the bed and scoots closer to me. I can feel the warmth radiating from him. I look over as he starts to draw, and his thick, midnight black hair has fallen around his face. God, what I would do to this man. Good Lord, Olive, get a hold of yourself. Before I can stop myself, I reach over and brush the hair back from one side of his face. He turns and looks at me, eyes full of hunger. I swallow, look down quickly, and comment on his drawings.

“These are very good. They do look familiar. We are working on an exhibit at the museum that may have some information that I can use to help us.”

“At the museum, with Mark?” he asked with what sounds like jealousy.

“Yes. He is on my team at work, and we have become fast friends outside of work, too. I'm actually going out with him and a few others when I wake up.”

“Then I must prolong your waking up. I do not like this male taking you from me.”

“Excuse me? No one is taking me from you. Mark is my friend too, and I will be seeing him, and you will not stop me. I am so tired of everyone expecting me to bow down to them!” Go me! Now if I could just do that with my family!

“I am sorry, Olive. I have overstepped. Of course, you have more to your life than me. You are all I have had for hundreds of years, and I have become possessive and forgotten myself. Please do not be angry at me.” He isn’t saying it to make me feel bad, but damn I feel like shit now. No, it needed to be said but shit! A man apologizing? Why could he not be in my waking life? Ugh!

"It's okay. I just have never had friends who actually cared about me before and I really like it. I don't want to lose that. I don't want to lose you either, okay." I say, putting my hand on his cheek. He looks at me with those silky black eyes, and I am weak as he puts his hand on the back of my head. He leans down, and...my alarm goes off. FUCK.

I wake up very frustrated. I turn over and a hand immediately goes to my face. "As much as I may want to be able to see you," he caresses my face, letting me know he understands, and then tucks my hair behind my ear. "I need to get up and get ready. I won't be out late. It is just brunch." I pick up the recorder, "I promise I will be back soon."

"My Olive, I…I hope you enjoy your time with your friends," he says in his sexy, husky voice. It feels like there is more he wants to say but decides not to, and I don't push. Instead, I thank him and get up to get ready.

I choose to wear a black, wide legged jumpsuit with a plunging neckline, tied waist, and long sleeves. I wear my hair in loose curls pulled back on one side with a comb. I look in the bathroom mirror. Yep, I look good. I walk into my room to put on my black strappy heels, and the door closes behind me. Suddenly, there are hands on my waist. "I guess you think I look good," I giggle, "I really do have to go though. I will see you in just a bit. I promise."

I pull up to The Loft and head to The Bunch & Bitch area. Mark and the others are there and are all smiles when they see me. I feel a buzz of excitement at the thought of everyone being happy to see me. I could get used to this. Of course, Candy is obsessed with my outfit. Even Jennifer pipes up and asks if we can go shopping together because she loves my style. That makes me feel really good because she is at least four sizes smaller than I am. I hate that I think that way. I really need to stop that. It doesn't matter what size anyone is. Everyone deserves to have confidence and wear what makes them feel good, even me. Mark leans over.

"You do look gorgeous, Olive." He gives me a wink and a slight rub on my back. I feel so good today. Everything is going well so far. I am surrounded by people I care about and who care about me. Plus, I am finally beginning to feel comfortable in my skin. Yeah, today is a good day.

We are having a blast at brunch. This show is so hilarious, and I'm wildly impressed with all the makeup, and admittedly, jealous of the queens. I ordered a specialty cocktail, the Werk-It Whiskey Sour, and I'm definitely copying this one at home! I am so glad I came with the group today. I really needed this. Maybe I could start to trust my friends enough to confide in, especially Mark. Not today, but soon. I will open up. That is a goal I am going to set for myself. To open up to a friend, at least a little. We all walk to our cars. Mark walks me to mine and hugs me before going to his car. I get into mine and notice I have several missed calls from Granddad and my aunt.

I call the lesser of the two evils. Granddad answers and tells me that he had to take Grandmother to the hospital for drinking bleach.

"What? Why?" I ask.

"We don't really know. She said it was an accident, but the doctors don't believe her and want to put a hold on her," he replied. Honestly, I didn't disagree with them at all. How does one not…know...they…oh god, she may have had a little help with that bleach.

"Do you need me to come up there?"

"No, it may just agitate her. I just wanted to let you know what was going on. She may be here for a week or so under medical and psychiatric monitoring."

"Okay. If you need me to do anything, let me know."

With that, we hang up. I head home and hope what I am thinking is not true. Even if it is, am I mad? Not really. What does that say about me? Do I want her dead? No, but do I care about anything else? I think about that as I pull into the driveway. As soon as I get in the door, I feel him near me. My heart feels like it skips a beat. Corny as hell but also true. He is so close. His earthy, woodsy scent is all I can sense.

"Please tell me you didn't give her bleach to drink," I halfheartedly beg. I feel his warm cheek against mine as he turns his head from side to side. No, he didn't. "You know what happened, though?" I ask. He moved his head up and down. I stand there with his face against mine. I can feel his breath on my neck with him this close. Shivers run through my body. I have it bad for this no-ghost dude, and from what I am feeling, he is feeling the same way for me. Reluctantly, I say, “I need to get changed and do some more research for you.” He backs up and follows me upstairs.

Chapter 16: HIM

I am drawing the symbols, and suddenly, I feel her touch, and I turn to her. I am lost in her pale blue eyes that ignite something primal in me. Before I can act on my feelings, she looks away and comments on my pictures. Damn. I fear something bad has happened in her past, and I do not want to act fast, but I want to kiss her perfect, lush lips.

I do not mean to upset her about keeping her here with me. I am just so enamored with her. I want to spend every one of my moments with her. I know her friends are important to her, but why does one have to be this male that makes her smile when he sends her messages? When she puts her hand on my face, it's too much. I place my hand on the back of her head and neck to pull her to me. I lean down into her, and then her damn alarm wakes us up.

I want to tell her so much about how I am feeling. How more and more every day I am falling for her, and never have I been more desperate to find a way to free myself so I can be with her. Instead, I tell her to have fun with her friends. Idiot. I am an idiot.

She walks back into the room dressed like a goddess. I cannot help myself. I close the door and grab her by the waist before I could think better of it. She lets out the most glorious laugh my ears have ever heard, and I cannot help but to smile. Before I know it, she is out the door, though off to Mark.

I sulk downstairs and see the hag fussing at the old man as he looks around her to see the television. I need to get revenge for my Olive. As much as it disgusts me, I will follow this despicable woman around and make her miserable. Eventually, she gives up trying to get his attention and goes to the kitchen for coffee. I was getting ready to start opening doors when I noticed her looking like she was plotting. While it doesn't surprise me this witch would plan something sly and manipulative, I was curious what she was doing. Next thing I know, she has her coffee on the counter, with a bottle of creamer and a bottle of bleach beside it. She runs out of the kitchen screaming that she drank the bleach in her coffee. She absolutely did not drink the bleach. What the hell is she doing?

The old man jumps from his chair and gets her to sit down while he calls an ambulance. As he goes to get the phone, she sits there and smiles. Smiles. All of this is for attention. Never have I seen this in all my years, and I have seen many things. This is very odd, evil even. I don't understand this behavior and this is why I despise humans. They are all disgusting, little creatures. Well, all but my Olive, but she is a goddess among her kind. The old man comes back in and the liar begins to cry again, saying she mistakenly put bleach in her coffee instead of creamer and then drank it. He hugged her and tried to comfort her, as she was increasingly "upset". The ambulance arrived and the old man followed in his truck. Now I am here alone until Olive gets home. It never really bothered me before; it was just my existence, but since I saw Olive, all I want is to be free and be with her, protect her, and show her the love she deserves. I would do anything to make that happen. The loneliness when she is not here is overwhelming. It's all consuming. The silence is deafening.

I hear Olive pull up to the house, and I am ready at the door for her to walk in. I stand so close to her that all I smell is him. Mark. This will not do at all. I do not like this. Before my anger can take over, she asks if I knew about the liar's situation. I lean in cheek to cheek with her and answer with a nod and a shake of the head. This also rids her of the male's scent. She seems satisfied with my answers, so we head up towards her room.

We go into her room and she grabs some night clothes and heads to the bathroom to change. She comes back in and is hardly wearing anything. She has a small top and shorts. Is she trying to torture me? If she is, she is doing a wonderful job. She picks up the recorder.

"Okay, so can you tell me what she did?" Olive asks. So, I tell her everything. She makes a huffing noise.

"Why does this not surprise me? Every so often, when she isn't getting enough attention or is having man trouble, she pulls stunts like this, and everyone fawns over her for a while." She rolls her eyes. "She's quite the attention whore."

I raise my eyebrows at that and as if she can see me, she smirks as she shrugs her shoulders and gives a cheeky giggle.

"Now that is out of the way, I had an idea. I thought since you can manipulate physical items, maybe you could draw the symbols in our waking world so I would have them to reference during research."

"I believe I can do that. Before that though, I must tell you how exquisite you look today. Before and now. You are breathtaking." I gently caress a finger down her arm. God, she is so soft.

"Thank you. I felt good today, and you helped with that," she said with a warm smile.

I put my hand to her face and lean in to kiss her. I get a breath from her, and she says, "No, wait," my heart drops, "I want this too, but I want to see you. Let's do some research and I promise we will kiss when we dream tonight." She does not have to tell me twice.

"Where is the paper and pencil?" I say quickly and she laughs as she gathers what we need. She chats about her day and I clench my jaw every time she brings up Mark. I will say her friends do sound like they are good to her. That is good because if they were not, I would hunt them down when I am freed. I draw the few symbols I remember and Olive is delighted. I would do anything to see that smile.

"This is wonderful! You are so talented! I will take this to work tomorrow and compare it to some samples. We have to see if there is a match."

"You need dinner and then sleep," I tell her.

"I was thinking we could skip to the sleeping part," she says with a smirk.

Again, I do not need to be told twice.

Chapter 17: OLIVE

I open my eyes and turn over, and it barely registers that he is there when his lips crash into mine. This is no timid kiss. This is heat and weeks of unspoken tension exploding at once. This kiss is life changing. We moved together in a perfect, frantic rhythm. Nothing outside us exists. My hands are fisted on his tunic while his fingers tangle in my hair as we slow our pace. We are lying here, peppering each other with kisses and hands roaming over each other's bodies. Each touch is a confession. Every kiss is a promise. He looks at me, so full of wanting and love, and I melt. I am falling hard and fast. He will be the end of me. I will do anything to be with him.

"I am sorry I moved so fast, Olive. When you said you would kiss me, it has been all I have thought of," he said.

"Don't be sorry. That was amazing. I wanted you to kiss me. Just like that," I say with a smile. He smiles back with the most devastatingly handsome smile, and I know I am definitely done for.

"I want more, Olive. I want all of you. Only when you are ready, I sensed something when you were near the male Steve, and I will not pressure you," a consent king and observant. Swoon.

"Yes, there are some things in my past that make me uncomfortable around certain people. You are not one of those people. You do everything you are supposed to. You make me comfortable, seen, and safe."

"Would you tell me those things? You do not have to, but I would listen and help if I can."

"The last time I told anyone besides my therapist, they accused me of lying and did nothing to stop it."

"I know you do not lie, my Olive."

I tell him everything. I mean everything. Starting with my parents, my grandparents, my mental health struggles, everything. Dream me has no problem opening up. Then again, maybe it's just because it's him. I feel safe with him. Perhaps it's because he can't tell anyone or gang up against me. No. I don't think he would do any of those things anyway. I think he genuinely cares. He gets agitated a few times and has to pace to calm himself, but he insists he is okay and wants to know everything I have been through.

"No one has defended you?"

"No. I think I'm an easy target, and I keep Grandmother's attention off everyone else."

"This will not do. I will defend you now."

"You have already, with the pots and pans and the paint spilling. I really appreciate it too."

"I will be more vigilant. No one will harm you." He puts a hand on my cheek and kisses me softly.

“Thank you. Enough bad stuff. Let's talk about some happier things, please. Is there anything you want to know about me?”

“I know about you. You love to read. When you read naughty scenes, your cheeks turn pink.” His lips curve upward mischievously before continuing. “You love old things. You love to watch the stars, and you like to run. Your favorite color is green, but not just any green. It's a green called dark emerald, like the gem. Your favorite sandwich is something called cajun ham with mayonnaise, mustard, lettuce, and tomato. Shall I go on?” he says with a smirk.

“When is my birthday? How old will I be?” I say sassily.

“October 31 and you will be 28.”

“Fine, Mr. Observant. What about you? What do you like to do? What’s your favorite color?”

“Honestly, before I met you, all I did was pester humans until they left my space. And I existed miserably alone. Then, I saw you and everything changed. I do not want to be alone anymore. I also no longer hate all humans. I want to be better for you, Olive. I want to find a way to be free to be with you. As for my favorites, my color is the icy blue of your eyes. My favorite scent is you. That intoxicating, light lavender and vanilla aroma. My favorite taste…Well, I have not tasted it yet, but I know it will be you.”

That is all the warning I get before his lips are on mine again. There was no rush. No need to prove anything. Just electricity, hearts beating too fast. It was a kiss that said I want you, but also, I see you. It lingered in the air after it ended.

"Will you hold me?" I ask with our foreheads pressed together.

"Of course, my Olive."

I lie down in his arms with my head on his chest, and inhale his scent before my eyes open.

Chapter 18: Olive

The following week flew by. It was the best week, too. Work has been great. Home has been great. My time with him has been better than great. Did I mention everything has been great? Since it is the first weekend in October, the group has decided to go to Salem for the weekend. Fortunately, I get to avoid Grandmother coming home. But I am going to miss him so bad. He is not happy that I am leaving for the weekend, but he understands that this is important to me. I brought my bag with me this morning so we could leave after work today. He showered me with kisses in bed, while I dressed, while I put on my shoes. I think he may miss me a little bit. We still have only kissed. I have a feeling he is holding back because of my history. I may have to take the lead on this one.

I am rooming with Mark while in Salem, so we decided to ride together too. As we ride, we talk. We talk about life, dating, family, and I actually do open up a little bit. I am super proud of myself. I tell him about how Grandmother always tries to embarrass me and make me feel bad for the way I look. I even tell him about the time that she switched out my vitamins with pepper pills. She laughed and said, "Beauty is pain," when I doubled over in pain. I was 10 years old.

"Olive. Seriously, is she jealous or something? You are stunning! What is her deal? I am so sorry you have had to deal with that cruelty growing up."

"Thanks. I think it's because I look so much like my mom, and she blames her for my dad leaving the family."

"That is not your fault. You need to get out of that environment. I have a spare room at my house. I could totally rent it to you."

"Honestly, that does sound appealing. I need to think about it. The entire reason I'm staying with my grandparents is to save money for a place of my own.

"Please think about it, Olive. You are too good to be dealing with that." He pulls my hand up and kisses it.

We pull up to The Witch's Inn. Why stay in Salem if you don't stay in a haunted hotel? And of course, we booked the most haunted room. Mark gets us checked in, and we head to our room. We enter, and there is one problem. There's only one bed.

"I can go see if there is a room with two beds, if that would make you more comfortable," Mark suggests.

"No. That's okay, unless you're uncomfortable." I reply.

"Why would sharing a bed with a beautiful woman make me uncomfortable?" I shoot him a look and we both laugh.

We meet up with the others and have dinner at a local diner. Then, we all go to an old cemetery and walk around the graves. The spooky vibe is thrilling and eerie at the same time. After we finish our stroll amongst the dead, we head back to our hotels for the night.

I warn Mark, I am going to wash my face and use a mask, so I am going to look hideous. He insists that it is impossible and tells me to put it on him, too, so we will match. We put on our masks, and honestly, we both look ridiculous, and I love it. We order some dessert from room service and chat while we dig in. Once we both start yawning, we decide to settle in for the night.

Sometime during the night, the blankets get pulled off of us and end up on the floor. Apparently, this is a claim for the room. We wake up, snuggled up to each other, and laugh at how the ghost is trying to play matchmaker.

We join the others for breakfast and relay our story. We are met with kissy sounds and giggles. We all laugh and start talking about what's up for the day. We go to a couple of museums, but mostly shop at all the quirky little stores in the area. By the time dinner rolls around, we are famished. We stop at a pizza shop and get a couple of pizzas and some beer. We have a wonderful time chatting about everything and nothing. The walk back to the hotel is nice. The streets are a buzz with the excitement of Halloween approaching. We walk quietly and slowly down the street. When Mark offers his arm, I take it.

The hour and a half ride back is too short. I am not looking forward to seeing Grandmother again. This weekend was so lovely. I didn't want it to end. Maybe I should take Mark up on his offer. We pull up to my car. Mark puts my bags in and gives me a hug. He takes my hand, "Think about my offer, Olive. You don't even have to pay rent. I just want you safe and away from her." "Thank you, Mark. I will think about it." With that, I get in the car and head home.

I pull in the driveway and notice my aunt and Steve are there. Great. I walk in and immediately am hit with his scent and kisses on my neck. I have to pretend it is not happening because my grandmother is standing in the foyer in front of the stairs.

"Hello, Olive. I want to apologize for how I treated you the last time I saw you. I feel better now, and I wanted to say that." With that, she walks away.

My aunt walks in, and I ask, "What is up with her?"

"She is heavily medicated! Isn't it great!" and she walks away. Well, okay then. I go up the stairs, eager to be alone with him again.

I get in my room and lock the door. Steve is here, and I don't exactly get innocent vibes from him. I feel safer with the door locked. I go and I grab the recorder. Strong arms pull me in, and I am again being peppered with kisses.

"I'm taking it that you missed me a little bit?"

"You jest, Olive, but these were the worst three days of my life. I never want to be without you. You are my life. You are my heart. You are my Olive." Okay, way to make me feel guilty.

"I'm sorry it was so bad for you. I do have good news, though."

"What…is…it?" he asks between kissing me.

"I found out where the symbols are from." That got his attention.

"I knew you could, Olive. You are so intelligent."

"They are from a tribe that lived in areas all around here, called First Nations."

"That name sounds familiar, but it is just out of my mind's reach."

"That's ok. We will figure this out. I even have Mark helping me a little."

"Mark? No. No Mark. I said nothing, but you smelled of him when you came home."

"Well, about that. We drove together and stayed in the same room."

"In the same bed?" he says, sounding agitated.

"I am not going to lie to you. Yes, but nothing happened. No touching at all. It's not like that." An angry, rage filled aura surrounded the room, and then, he was gone. Well, shit.

The rest of the evening I spent downstairs with my family, and Grandmother was on her best behavior. I even ate in peace. No comments. Maybe all she needed was some mental health care. She has had it before, but she used it more like a vacation and only stayed to get attention. Then, when she was satisfied, she said what needed to leave. This time it seems different.

He never came to me when I went back to my room. I stayed up later waiting for him. Eventually, sleep took over, and still, he did not come.

Chapter 19: HIM

Kissing her is my new favorite thing to do. When she turned over and looked at me, whatever thread of self control I had snapped. I crash into her mouth with fire and possession. There is nothing careful in this kiss, and she is giving me back everything I am giving her. She wants this as much as I do, and that only intensifies my need for her. My feelings for her are strong and get stronger every day. I want to tell her, but I am afraid she will not feel the same way.

We talk for a while, and she tells me of her past. I know this is extremely difficult for her to do, so I try to keep my composure. I find that almost impossible to do, considering the horrendous things that have been done to my sweet Olive. I pace back and forth, trying to tamp down my anger. I want to raze everyone to the ground that ever hurt her. She tells me I cannot, but if I could, I would do so. She changes the subject and is surprised when I notice all the things about her. Does she not believe me when I tell her how I feel? I must do a better job at that. I do not lie when I say all my favorite things. Before her, there were no favorite things. Now, there is only her.

For the next week, she spends her days at work trying to decipher the symbols I drew, and her nights are spent with me. We talk, read, do research, and of course, my favorite, kiss. Without question, I would like to do more, but only when she is ready. One night, she says the words that make my heart stop. She is going out of town with Mark for three days. In truth, she is going with a group, but all I care about is Mark. I try to be supportive, but it is challenging. A wave of unease washes over me, and I feel like I will lose her.

She left today. I already feel her absence in my soul. When I thought things could not get worse, the old, shriveled hag walks in. At first, I begin to rush her and push her, but something is off. Her demeanor is different. Dulled, diluted. Hmm, this is something to watch. The old man comes in behind her and has her sit. He goes and begins a task in the kitchen. I stay and watch the woman. She stares at the television, yet it is not on. Ha, idiot. I go and switch it on, hoping to scare her. She says thank you before sitting back and watching it. Well, this is no fun. This new version of the hag is uninteresting. The old man returns with some medication and a glass of water. She takes it from him and leans back in her seat. Ahh, she is being subdued on purpose. Good. This is a pleasing change. She needs it.

The following two days pass slowly and without incident, as I count down the hours until Olive comes home. I do hope she is having fun. I wish I could be with her. The sooner we can break this curse, the better. I want to be free, to be with her. I want everyone to see us together. I want to love her properly. I want to make her happy.

A few hours before she is due home, the old couple's daughter comes over to check on her mother. Then the sleazy male, Steve, comes by. They decide to cook a meal. I know Olive will dread this because of the old zombie of a woman and the unsettling male, but I will try my best to shield her from them.

Finally, she pulls into the driveway. I meet her at the door. I immediately pull her into my arms and begin kissing her neck. I know she loves this. I know she cannot acknowledge me, but I cannot resist. I do not realize the witch is behind me until it speaks and apologizes, not for everything, but for one occasion. I am not convinced. Something is amiss. At the moment, I do not care. My girl is home, and I need to get her upstairs.

She closes the door and gets the recorder. I pull her in and begin kissing her again. I can't help it. I am crazy about her. She teases me about missing her, and I tell her some of my feelings for her. She doesn't say them back, which is why I do not tell her everything. It would hurt too badly. So, I will give her more time. Then she says something that interests me. She has found the tribe the symbols belong to. We are one step closer to freeing me, and then we can be together out in the world. Then, it is like she splashes me with cold water and brings up Mark. She tells me they shared a room and a bed in Salem. She says more but I cannot hear her over the roaring in my ears. I feel full of anger and rage. I have to get out of here. I do not want to hurt her. I rush out and leave her standing there. I speed through the house, bumping into the creep as I go by, causing his eyes to go wide. I head to the garage. I have not been here in months. I have desired staying close to Olive, but for now, I need to keep my distance. I go into the storage room and slam the door.

How could she do this? She knows my sentiments toward this male. I feel betrayed. Does she not have any feelings for me? Do our kisses mean nothing to her? Does our time together mean nothing to her? I long to be with her, but when I am free, would she even want to be with me? She slept in the bed with him as she does with me. Does that mean nothing to her? Even with all these questions and feelings of betrayal, sadness, and rage, I still want her. I cannot give in. So, I stay in this room.

After I am sure she is asleep, I go to check on her. Does she miss me? Does she even notice I am not there? Does she dream of him? I need to rid myself of this built up energy, so I go downstairs and release some by making the electricity flicker. It only eases the pressure a little, but to a manageable amount. The old man curses and mumbles something about an electrician.

The next week is the worst. I have not spoken to Olive. Although she has tried, and I admit, I check on her often. I am beyond hurt. I do not know how to recover from this. I am in her room watching her try to do more research for me. Even now, she is trying to help me. Is that something, right? She picks up the recorder.

"Please, I can feel you here. Please say something."

"Hello, my Olive," She loosens a shaky breath and tears up.

"Hi. I have missed you. I am so sorry. I should have insisted on two beds. I promise nothing happened."

"I believe you, Olive. I have missed you. I should have trusted you. I just felt betrayed. I know you do not feel as deeply for me as I do you, and I had no right to act that way."

"First of all, your feelings are valid. You felt that way, and that's okay. Second, I do feel that way about you. This past week has been hell without you."

Hearing those words soothe the sadness I have been carrying. I grab her and hold her like I will never let go. I may not.

"Let's go to bed. I need to see you."

Chapter 20: Olive

I turn over and face him. God, I have missed him. I pull him in for a kiss. Our lips meet slowly, softly. It is tender at first, and then deepens as he slides his hand to my cheek. I curl my fingers into his tunic, and the kiss grows into something warmer, fuller. Into everything we have been holding back. Everything between us is charged and heavy. I trace a slow path up his arm under his tunic. His eyes darken with a primal lust and want.

"Tell me to stop, Olive," he says in a low, rough voice.

"I won't."

"Fuck."

Our lips meet with even more urgency than last time, full of heat and longing. His hands slip around my waist and pull me flush against him, and I can feel how much he wants me. I melt even more into his kiss and slide my fingers into his hair. As we move together, our clothes become obstacles. His fingers pull at the hem of my shirt. I raise my arms, giving silent permission, and he does the same. He flips me on my back and hovers over me. I arch beneath him, and he traces kisses along my throat and collarbone, pausing to bite down enough to make me gasp.

His fingers slide down my body, and he begins slowly pulling off my panties until I am writhing beneath him.

"Tell me what you want, Olive."

"You. Now. Hard."

He gives a smirk that is pure danger as he pulls off his pants, freeing his large, impressive cock. He pushed into me in one smooth thrust, and my cry split the quiet. Our bodies move like wildfire, fast, consuming, unstoppable. Sweat slicks our skin as pleasure builds for both of us, sharp and brutal. Our climaxes crash over us, leaving us trembling and tangled in the sheets. He rolls to his side and pulls me into him. He doesn't let go, and I don't want him to.

My head lies on his chest, rising and falling with the breaths he takes. He idly traces circles on my shoulder, like he can't stop touching me. I have never felt so cared for. Neither of us spoke for a while. Words don't feel necessary right now. Finally, I look up at him and ask,

"Are you okay?"

"I am better than okay, my Olive," he said, placing a kiss into my hair.

I sigh with contentment as I nestle closer. Something more than sex is different between us. Something unspoken but understood. I wonder if he is feeling the same way I do.

I wake up in the morning still wrapped in his arms. I do not want to get up, but I need to get to work, so I place a kiss on his chest since I can't see his face now, and head to the shower. I look in the mirror, and there on my collarbone is a bite mark. What the hell? Okay, that's new. What happens in dreamstate carries over to real life now. I head back to my room to finish getting dressed. No need for modesty now. I am getting out some pants, and I feel a slap on my bottom. I laugh and am pulled back into a muscular chest, and he kisses my head. "I can't wait to get home to you later. Hopefully, I will have some more information on the symbols and the tribe they came from." He pulls me in for one more kiss, and then I am off. I could get used to this. Well, with him free so I can see him all the time.

I walk down the stairs with him closely behind me. As I walk into the kitchen, I see that Grandmother is here. I brace myself for the inevitable insults, and I feel him tense behind me. She only smiles, says good morning, and walks out. Okay, something is up. This is not the same woman I grew up with. I know meds can help a great deal to manage symptoms, but not to alter your entire personality. I don't have time to worry about this right now. So, I grab my water bottle from the counter and leave for work.

"What are these symbols for again?" Mark asks.

"I found them during a late night research session and thought that the museum may have more information on them. I know they are from the First Nations tribe, but other than that, I have not had much luck. Since the First Nations people lived in the area, I thought it could be useful for a new exhibit."

"I got you. That sounds like a great idea. Let's see what we can find."

"Thank you so much for indulging me. I really do believe this could lead to something bigger."

"Maybe we will make a discovery, strike it rich, move away, and live happily ever after."

"Seriously? Happily, ever after?" I laugh.

"Hey, a man can dream. Can't he?" he says with a laugh and a shrug of his shoulders.

After a while, we are not having any luck. This is more difficult than I thought it would be. Are these attached to whatever spell or curse that is tying him to that land? Mark suggests a lunch break, and I happily agree.

"I have never seen anything like it, Olive. There is just nothing. Usually, there is something to lead us in some kind of direction, but it is like these were purposely erased from history."

"I get that feeling too. Why, though? I just don't get it." I reach my hand into my purse for my phone. It's not there. Shit. I left it on my bedside table this morning.

"Is everything ok?"

“Yeah, I left my phone at home today and just realized it.”

“Oh, expecting a hot text?” he says with a playful wink.

“I wish! Nope, just a habit to check for it. I'm boring like that.” I laugh.

“Olive, you are anything but boring, darling.” he flashes one of his best smiles. He is so cute.

We finish up at the museum for the day and still have no new leads, but we did get some research done on other tribes we are working on. Mark walks me to my car and gives me a hug goodbye. I have this nagging feeling that something is off at home, but I push it aside and focus on getting home to him.

I walk in the door and start up the stairs to him when Grandmother calls out to me from the living room. I reluctantly go to her. Her hair is pulled back, and she is actually dressed today. She is holding my phone out to me. What the hell?

“You left this in the kitchen this morning. I held on to it for you.”

“Oh, thank you. You look good, like you're feeling better.”

“Yes, I am feeling much better. Thank you for noticing,” she says. It comes out a bit strained, like she doesn't want to be speaking to me. Yep, something is definitely up with her.

"Did you look at my phone? It's unlocked and I normally," she interrupts me,

"No, Ollie. I wouldn't do that." She totally would do that.

"Ok, I'm sorry, Grandmother. Have a good night." She definitely looked at my phone. What is she up to? I turn away and go up to my room. He is there waiting to scoop me up as soon as I get in. I go to grab the recorder and notice the drawer is open on my bedside table. I know that I left that closed. Maybe he remembered something today and needed to get more drawing supplies while I was gone.

"Hi, did you miss me?

"Always, my Olive," he says as I feel his hands on my waist.

"You smell like the other male," he said, stepping back.

"Oh no, sir, do not do that. Mark gave me a hug goodbye. That is all. We are just friends."

"I believe and trust you. It is other males I do not trust," he says, stepping back into me.

"We did a lot of digging today and still cannot find anything on those symbols. It's like they were erased from all the tribe's history."

“If they were part of my curse, they may have been. Are there any living elders left today?”

“I haven't gotten that far yet, but that is a great idea. I will look into it.”

“Olive, can you get ready for bed?”

“Oh, someone is wanting a repeat performance?” I say with a laugh.

“I have a feeling every time will feel like the first with you, my Olive. Now, please lock the door and get in bed.” He doesn’t have to tell me twice.

Chapter 21: HIM

This human who has captured all of me will be my ruin. I know this. I accept this gladly. Anything for her. I am madly, deeply in love with Olive. I could not have stopped it if I had wanted to. She slipped into my world of darkness like sunlight through a window. Warm. Quiet. Each day, warming the cold exterior that I had built up. For me, I cannot go back. There is only forward. There is only her.

When Olive leaves for work, it is either gone upstairs and wait for her or watch the others. When the old man clicks the television on, I decide that it may be worth looking at. Maybe he will pick a show like before. One that will help me remember something new. So far, no such luck. He is watching a show about car mechanics. This does not interest me. I go to rise, and the old shrew walks in from the direction of Olive's stairs. She rarely goes up there, but there is another room there, so it is possible she was in there. Olive locks her door anyway. I do notice that she is much more nicely dressed than she has been, and there is an air about her that has not been there in weeks. The old man tells her it is time for her medication and gives it to her. She immediately announces she has to go to the bathroom and disappears for a bit. I would not think anything of it except that I have observed this behavior over the last week. I must mention it to Olive. She returns with a notebook and pen and begins writing. Perhaps she journals like Olive. As I walk by her, I knock the notebook to the floor just to see her eyes go wide, and I walk away.

The old man is in the garage working on his latest project, his truck. I am not sure what he is doing, but he uses much colorful language, and his anger is palpable. I have become much too calm, so I like to still feed on that anger from time to time. And I may give him a little push sometimes. Just because I love Olive does not mean I do not hate the other humans. Just as he is reaching the spot he has been trying to get to, I make his headlight go out, and a slew of curses I have never heard come from under the hood of the truck. Oh, that was fun. Lights flash in the garage doors. My girl is home. I head to her room to greet her when she comes up.

I will never get used to the sight of her. She enters the room like a breeze of fresh air. I know she was meant for me. I miss her immensely when she is gone. She smells of the male, Mark. I do not like this at all. It makes me angry, but she assures me that there is absolutely nothing between them. I must trust her. We talk about the symbols. She said she has not made any progress, but I know if anyone can, it is her.

All I can think about is getting her into my arms. So, I suggest she gets ready for bed, and she, to my pleasure, wastes no time in locking the door. She begins to peel her clothing off, painfully slow. I go to assist. “No, sir. Sit on the bed and watch,” she commands. This is agonizing. I want my hands on her now. I reach out for her, and she swats me away. Her movements were unhurried in their lazy confidence. She trails her fingers along the hem of her shirt and pulls it slowly up her body, exposing her soft skin that I am aching to touch. She pulls it over her head and tosses it to the floor. She reaches behind her, unhooks her bra, and lets it fall to the floor as she walks toward me on the bed, swaying her hips deliberately while taking her time. She unzipped her skirt and let it fall to the ground; she is not wearing panties. I am about to come undone when she whispers, “Let's go to bed.”

We wake up in our dreamstate and I am on her. I cannot wait. This kiss was not gentle nor slow but full of intensity. I want to memorize her mouth, the way she sighs against me, the way she feels in my arms. Her hands find my shoulders, then my neck, then my hair, and she is pulling me as close as she can, like she cannot get enough. I begin kissing down her body, and she whispers a moan like it is a prayer, and that only adds to my arousal.

I slide between her legs and she tries to close them. “No. I told you that you will be my favorite meal. Now let me taste you.” She obeys. “Good girl, Olive,” I take my time teasing, tasting, learning what makes her make those breathy little sounds that are driving me wild. With every flick of my tongue, the careful pause has her lifting her hips off the bed and her fingers tangle into my hair. Her breath becomes ragged and uneven. I stay right there, driving her over the edge until she finally falls apart on my tongue.

I lay beside her and pull her into me, “I could do that all night. You taste so sweet, my Olive.” She looks up at me and pulls my face down to hers and begins to kiss me. What begins as a lazy, slow kiss quickly turns into a passionate inferno. This is not just lust. This is deeper than that. This is desperate, raw. She sits up, and at first, I do not know what she is doing until she climbs atop of me to straddle me. I line myself up to her entrance and grab her by the hips. I move her down slowly, letting her feel every inch of me. Letting myself feel her. Her eyes roll back towards the ceiling and she moans one of those breathy moans I love so much and it takes all I have not to come. When she is fully atop of me, I move her hips, deepening the rhythm as we go. She tilts her head back and moans louder with pleasure. We were everywhere together, around each other, connected more than just physically. Our movement becomes more frantic as we chase the pleasure building. We come apart together. She looks at me and I cannot believe that she is real. I never want this moment to end.

We lay there, tangled up together in the sheets for a while in silence. No words are needed and the silence is anything but awkward. I lie there with the truth of my feelings sitting in my throat. They are heavy, real and only for her. As if sensing my drifting thoughts,

"Are you okay?" she asks, looking up at me.

"Yes, I am. I have something I want to tell you."

"Okay, you are kind of scaring me. Is it bad?"

"No, it is the opposite or at least for me it is."

"Okay…"

"I love you, my Olive. I have since the day you came here. It was like a lightning strike to the heart, sudden and electric." The silence that follows has my heart hammering in my chest. Time does not slow. It vanishes. She does not feel the same way. My chest tightens. I look away.

Chapter 22: Olive

He loves me. Me. How does someone as perfect as him love someone like me? No one loves me. He loves ME. HE LOVES ME! I realize my inner monologue has left a long silence, and he has looked away. I pull his face to me, and a tear rolls down his cheek, and I wipe it away. “Oh no, I’m sorry! I love you so much, it physically hurts, and I don't even know your name. I do not know why someone like you loves me, but” I pull him closer and whisper against his lips, “Oh, how I love you.” The kiss starts as a whisper on our lips, then he deepens the kiss, and for a second, I think we may go for round three. Instead, he pulls me in and just holds me close. I have to find a way to free him soon.

***

“I think I found a contact at the First Nations Museum in Burlington. That may be a place to get some answers on your symbols,” Mark says as we work sorting our artifacts.

“Mark, you are the best! I will call them today!”

“I thought you would like that. Kai is the one who runs things there, so ask for him.”

“Hey, Olive, there is a woman here wanting to see you. She says she is your grandmother,” Candy says as she pops her head in the room.

"Wonderful," I say sarcastically.

"I'm coming with you," Marks says, removing his gloves.

We walk to the lobby, and there she is in all her teased hair glory. I feel physically ill at the sight of her here in my place.

"HEY, Ollie!! So, this is where you work! Oh, who is this handsome fellow?"

"I'm Mark. Olive's friend." He says, placing his hand on the small of my back.

"Oh, perfect! Then you can come to Ollie's party, I am going to throw it for her birthday!"

"What party? What are you talking about?" I question.

"Well, I have been thinking that you have worked really hard, and I wanted to do something nice for you. Since your birthday is coming up, I thought a costume party at the house would be fun. Please say yes. I came here to invite your work friends to make sure you have a good turnout." Hmmm, that's it? No insult to go with that? I don't trust this.

"I don't know, Grandmother, I don't like to be the center of attention."

"I know, Ollie, but this would help me out, too. Steve and I are going to do an event planning business when interior design is slow." There it is. It benefits her.

"Olive, you can always think about it and let her know later today. You still have a week and a half to invite people." Mark interjects, and I shoot him a grateful look.

"Oh, of course, Ollie! I didn't mean to put you on the spot. Just let me know later!"

"Okay. I will, Grandmother. Thank you for coming by and thinking of me."

She nods and walks away. What the hell was that? What am I going to do? If I don't go through with this, she will be mad and be impossible to live with. If I go through with it, she very well may embarrass me in front of everyone. Ugh. Mark interrupts my thoughts with a suggestion of coffee and a chat. He knows me well.

"Do you think she could be being genuine? You have said she has been different since her hospital stay."

"Maybe, but my history with her suggests otherwise. There have been very few times she has celebrated my birthday, and the times she did, she would just humiliate me."

"She may just want to impress this Steve guy."

“That is possible. Actually, the only job she was ever good at was cake baking and decorating. She made a good living, too. Until she grew tired of it and got sloppy, on her final job she had, she was still decorating a wedding cake during the reception and was furious when they wouldn’t pay her!” We both died laughing at that. “There was this one birthday of mine that she baked me a cake, and after I ate a piece, she announced that the dog had licked all over it. I looked around and realized I was the only one who didn’t know, and I ran and threw up. When I came back, she said it was probably for the best. I didn't need to eat cake anyway.”

“Olive, why are you still there? Please come live with me.” Mark says, getting serious

“I just have a little longer and I can put a down payment on a house. Just a little longer.” I say to reassure Mark, but at this point, though, I am not sure I could leave HIM.

“I think I will have the party,” I say after a long pause.

“Why?”

“If I don't, she will make me miserable. Especially now that she has been to the museum. She will just come back. Besides, you can protect me from her.” I joke.

“You're damn right I will.”

We go back to the museum and invite our friends to the party. I must admit I am getting a little excited. Mark, Candy, Jennifer, and I decide to do a group costume of Alice in Wonderland. Mark will be Mad Hatter. Candy will be the White Rabbit. Jennifer will be coming as the Cheshire Cat. I will be Alice. We are going to have a shopping and dinner evening on Friday to get ready. Their excitement is contagious.

When I get home, he greets me at the door with a hug and neck kisses as usual. I can't wait to tell him about the new contact. Shit! I didn't actually call the new contact. I am so selfish. I got caught up in all the excitement of this party. First thing in the morning, I am making that call.

I walk into the living room to see Granddad in his chair in front of the television and Grandmother on the couch with Steve talking. She stops and looks at me when I walk in. "Hey, Ollie. Did you decide yet?"

I answer, "Yes. I would love to have a party. Thank you for thinking of me. I went ahead and invited everyone at work." This pleases her because she breaks out in a huge grin and claps her hands together.

"Wonderful!" Then she goes back to talking to Steve. I feel Steve's eyes on me as I leave the room. I just throw him a little wave and get to my room as fast as I can. I immediately lock the door.

As I turn around, I am pushed up against the wall, and I feel his breath on my neck and his hands roaming up my shirt. I have waited all day to be home with him again. I can't wait until he is free. OH!

"Hey, we had a breakthrough today with the symbols." He backs away just enough for me to grab the recorder.

"Mark found a man who runs a museum several hours from here. He may be able to help us figure them out. Isn't that wonderful?"

"It is, my Olive. There is nothing more that I want than to be free, to be with you all the time. To take you from this place and have a life of our own. I love you."

"I want all of those things, too. I love you so much."

"Olive, let's go to our dreams."

Chapter 23: HIM

We wake in our dream, holding each other, and I do not want to move. This is perfect. I am holding the one I love. The only thing that would make this complete would be to be free from this curse. That will happen. My girl is already making headway on that. With the help of Mark, albeit, but I guess I must be okay with that as long as I am free and with her.

I lie here holding her, our legs tangle naturally, and I gently trace circles on her arm. She sighs contentedly, and we both know this is precisely where we want to be. My fingers start to run through her soft hair.

"What are you thinking about?" she asks softly.

"Us. Our future. Waking up to you every morning. Sleeping next to you every night."

"Do you think you will still feel that way when you are free from your curse?"

"No." Her hand on my stomach stills. "I will feel stronger, deeper. I will always feel this for you. I will always be yours, if you will have me." She exhales a sigh of relief.

"Always." She smiles and nods, her voice barely a whisper.

After a while, I ask, "What is this party the old hag spoke of?"

"Old hag?" she said with a laugh.

"Yes. Hag, shrew, witch, bitch, ogress. Whatever you would like to call her." That made her laugh even harder. I could listen to the sound of her laughter all day.

"She is giving me a birthday party. I must admit, I am nervous about it. But you will be here and all of my friends, so hopefully it will be fun. Also, this is for her new job, apparently."

"New job? She was not good at her old decorating job, why would she be good at this one?" That really made her laugh. "Wait, will Mark be here?"

"Oh boy. Yes, he will be, and you WILL be nice! He is my friend, and he is helping with freeing you. Even if he doesn't exactly know it."

"I will behave as long as he does," I say with a huff.

"Just so you know, we are doing a group costume for the party. We are dressing up as characters from a book and movie called Alice in Wonderland."

"I have seen this where humans dress up on All Hallows Eve before. I have never been to a party, though. I also have never heard of Alice in Wonderland."

"You are in for a treat then. Parties can be fun. Hopefully this one will be. As for Alice in Wonderland, we can watch it this weekend if you would like. We could snuggle in bed and watch the movie until we fall asleep." She says, wagging her eyebrows. She is so adorable.

"That idea sounds wonderful, my Olive."

The rest of our time together, Olive tells me about her work at the museum, and I think about how one day I will be able to go see her important work preserving history. I am proud of her and the work she is doing. She tells me about her shopping trip with her friends, and I wish I could be right there beside her, matching her costume. I might look ridiculous, but I would do anything for her.

I tell her about the old man and the project on his truck and the little tricks I pull on him. She laughs and unenthusiastically scolds me. I tell her about how every time I walk by the old witch, I knock things over or slam a door, and she thinks that is VERY funny. I love to make her laugh, so I continue to tell her of my antics until it is time for us to leave the dreamstate. I give her one last kiss before we wake.

Chapter 24: Olive

It's Friday, and I finally got in touch with Kai. We have been playing phone tag this week and are finally able to speak to each other.

"I received your email with your drawings or the symbols, and while they are definitely from my tribe, I have never seen these particular ones before," Kai says.

"Why do you think it is so difficult to find their origins?"

"I am not entirely sure. There are many things that have been lost to time. As you know, with every culture, many of our stories and ways have suffered the same fate. I do have one more source that may be able to help us."

"That would be wonderful! I'm willing to do anything it takes to figure this out."

"My grandmother, Mali, is an elder in the tribe and may recognize these. However, she is out of town until next month. I can call her and fill her in. As soon as she gets back, we can meet and do more research if that works for you."

"That sounds like a great plan. Thank you so much for your help, Kai."

With that, we hang up. I wish I had more answers now, but at least I have a little more direction. I just wish it were sooner.

Our group decides to head home after work to change before meeting up to go shopping. Mark said he could swing by and pick me up since my house is on the way to the Halloween party store.

To my relief, I get into the house and up to my room unnoticed by Grandmother or Steve, who I hear "working" in the dining room. Once I enter my room, I lock the door behind me. I feel his presence before I feel his arms come around me. I love this feeling.

"I got in touch with my contact, and he thinks his grandmother may be able to help us."

"That is good news," he says after manipulating the recorder. He has gotten quite good at that without me having to do it. I like it. It's more like a real conversation that way.

"There is only one thing. She is out of town until next month. I was hoping for answers sooner. I want to be with you now."

"It will be okay, my Olive. A month is not that long. I thought you had dinner tonight."

"I do, but I came home to get ready…and it gave me a reason to be near you for a little while."

"I am glad you did," he says sweetly and then, more seriously, says, "I also need to tell you something I have noticed. The old bitch is acting strangely. She acts as though she is better and taking medications, but I have a feeling she is not. I have no proof. Just small signs and a feeling."

"I have a feeling too, but she is being really nice. Though it's almost too nice. I don't know what to think. I'm really confused about what is going on with her. I am trying to give her the benefit of the doubt because even though she has been so mean to me, I want her to see me and love me still."

"My sweet Olive," he says and kisses my forehead, "You should prepare yourself for your evening out."

I pull out a comfy light pink sweater and a pair of jeans and change. I feel his eyes on me, so I make sure I give a little show while I'm dressing just to tease him. I will pay for that later; well, I hope I do anyway. I check myself in the mirror and gather my things. I open the door and there stands Steve. Behind me, I hear a low growl.

"Um…hi…uh…can I help you?" I stutter.

"Your grandmother sent me up to ask your opinion on something for your party, but you look so beautiful I forgot what it was," he says, looking me up and down.

"OLLIE! YOUR HANDSOME FRIEND IS HERE!" calls Grandmother from downstairs. Not a moment too soon because I feel a rush of anger between me and Steve as I lock my door and run down the stairs.

Grandmother's smile turns into a scowl as she sees Steve stumble down the stairs behind me. I know exactly why he is stumbling and exactly who is pushing him. Mark looks like he is about to punch Steve until I pull him out the door.

"What the hell was that creep doing?"

"I don't know but he was making me uncomfortable. I don't want to talk about it."

"Olive…"

"Please, I just want to have fun. He will be gone by the time I get back."

Once we meet up with the others, things start feeling lighter again. After some fun looking at all the spooky Halloween things at the store, we all find our costumes. My Alice outfit is beautiful and a bit sexy. I think it is a little short, but the others assure me it is absolutely perfect on me. We look so good all dressed up together. I am really getting excited for this party. Maybe it will be a turning point for Grandmother and me.

After our fun shopping, we go out for dinner at this new seafood restaurant called The Salty Grill. They have this huge aquarium surrounding the dining room, and it really is something spectacular to see. We get the giggles over the irony of eating fish while being surrounded by fish.

"Well, I mean, it isn't like they are cousins or anything. This is salmon and they're tropical fish." Mark says.

"Yeah, different zip codes," I say. We all burst out in laughter again.

"That angelfish is staring at you, Candy. It may try to fight you." Jennifer jokes.

"Well, we are kind of having a dinner party at a fish crime scene." Candy replies. We all lose it again.

We finish up our meal and part ways for the evening. Mark drives me home and as we pull in the driveway, we see Steve is gone and all the lights are out.

"Olive, I know you don't want to talk about it and that is ok, but you know I am here, right?"

"I know and you don't know what that means to me. Really, Mark."

"Let me walk you to the door."

We both get out of the car and walk up to the house. He gives me a hug and a kiss on the head. We say goodnight as I unlock the front door. When I walk in, I do not feel him, so I quietly close and lock the door behind me and hurry to my room. Once I'm in, I put my things down and hang up my costume. Still, he isn't here. It is a lovely night and I decide to sit out on the deck and watch the stars, as I like to do sometimes. Maybe he will come out and join me. I grab a blanket and the recorder, hoping I will need it. I sneak through the house and manage to get outside without waking anyone. I wrap myself in the blanket, lie on the deck chair, and look up. The sky is clear tonight. It is so calm and peaceful. I feel him before he makes it to me, and he feels angry.

"Are you okay?" I ask, and then the recorder clicks.

"No."

"Do you want to talk about it?"

"I was worried about you. I wanted to comfort you. I wanted to defend you, but I cannot properly because I am not at my full power. I know this. I feel this. However, this Mark can. This Mark has your waking attention. This Mark hugs you. This Mark comforts you. This Mark kissed you. I saw it."

"You do comfort me. You do defend me as much as you can. In fact, you're the only one who has ever really defended me. We will get your power back as soon as we can. I promise. As for Mark, I promise he is just my friend. I swear this to you. It was an innocent kiss on the head from a concerned friend. Nothing more. I am so in love with you. I promise you have nothing to worry about."

"I feel helpless, and I hate it. It makes me angry. I want to hurt, to destroy, but I am limited. I do not understand any of it, and it makes me angrier. Know that I do not want to hurt you, though, Olive. I want to keep you safe. I want to make you happy."

"I feel safe when I am with you, and you make me very happy. Soon we will figure this out, and we can be together fully."

"Can I sit with you, Olive?"

"Of course. I would love nothing more."

He slides behind me, and I lean back against his chest. I pull the blanket up around us, and he wraps his arms around me. We sit watching the stars until we fall asleep.

Chapter 25: HIM

While Olive is at work today, the old man is watching one of his shows about the first people of these lands before the lands were taken from them. I sit and watch, hoping something will spur a memory. Everything seems so familiar yet not. It is like all the information is right at my fingertips, just out of reach. The man on the show begins to speak about medicine men and women, and I get a flash of long grey hair. As the show continues, I get a memory of chanting like a spell and fire, not a small fire, more like an inferno. I cannot wait until Olive comes home so I can tell her, and hopefully, this will aid her in our search.

Olive is home before her dinner, and I cannot wait to have her in my arms. I grab on to her as soon as she walks in. I turn on the recorder, which I am proud to say I have mastered. She has good news about our contact in New Hampshire, but they cannot get in touch with her for a month, which is not ideal, but I have no choice but to wait.

She is getting ready for her night out with her friends, and she is undressing and dressing at an excruciatingly slow pace. Oh, my naughty girl will pay for this later. I will not hinder her now, but when she returns, she is all mine.

When she opens the door to leave, the slimy male is in front of her. I quickly get between them in case he tries to touch her. I never want to see that fear in her face ever again. It makes me feel physically ill to know why she looks that way. Just before I go to shove him, the ear splitting shrill of the old woman sounds from downstairs, and Olive runs down towards the foyer. As Steve goes down the stairs, I give him a few pushes, and he continues to stumble. The old beast looks as though she has sucked on a lemon when she sees Steve behind Olive, and the male, who must be Mark, looks murderous. So, this is Mark. My mind drifts from the creep to this new male in my house. Mark. The just a friend. I do not like this at all. I have seen these models on television, and that is exactly what he looks like. No, I do not like this. Especially when Olive hooks her arm in his and walks out the door.

I am already in an obvious foul mood when I hear the squawking of the old bird and the snake male's voice.

"What was going on with you and Olive?"

"Oh, nothing, she asked me to help her with something in her room, but I told her I didn't feel comfortable without you there." THAT FUCKING LIAR!

"She is always trying to seduce men. As if she could, I mean, look at her."

"She isn't a bad looking girl; I just don't want her to get the wrong idea."

"Well, it's too bad she took after her mother; obviously, all the looks and fitness in the family came from me." Looks like she has not changed. This will break Olive's heart.

They head to the dining room to continue planning the party for next week. I am so filled with rage I can hardly see straight. I go to the kitchen, and before I can think, I pick up a knife and send it flying into the dining room. It narrowly misses the scumbag's head. Both of their eyes grow so large I think they may come out of their heads, and they run out of the room. Damn, I missed.

I go out to the garage and try to calm down, which does not happen. How could that old bitch not see through that sleazy male's lies? Why does she treat Olive so poorly? What is Olive doing? What is Mark doing to Olive right now? My brooding is interrupted by the old man.

"Listen, I know you're out here, I can feel you. I have made peace with you being here, but you can't throw knives at people." He knows I am here? He can feel my presence like Olive?

"I feel your anger, and I feel your calm when Olive is here. I am fine with it, but you have to behave in my house."

Fuck that, this is MY house, that is MY woman they are mistreating. I throw a wrench in his direction; he said no knives. He shakes his head and huffs, then walks out of MY garage.

After he leaves, I think about what he said about how he can sense me. There has to be something passed down from him to Olive that gives them the gift to sense beings like me. That is certainly interesting. That would explain Olive's and my easy connection with one another. My mind drifts back to her. The way she is treated makes me want to kill, even though I know that is not what she would want. The wrathful part of me does not care. I want to murder anyone who so much as looks in her direction including Mark. I wonder what they are doing. Is he making her laugh? Making her give him all the smiles meant for me? Is he touching her? Kissing her? I am so lost in thought I do not even sense she is home until I hear car doors shut. I go to the front stoop to greet her when I see him embrace her and kiss her. I cannot take this. If I stay here I will for certain kill this male. I rush back to the garage to prevent a massacre on the front steps.

When I calm down enough to go back out, I find Olive on the back deck watching the stars. She is completely enchanting. What male wouldn't be completely entranced by her?

She is wrapped in a thick blanket, and the recorder is beside her on a small table. Of course, she feels me there. She always does. She asks if I am okay. Of course, I am not ok. She could have been attacked tonight, and then I saw another kiss her. Albeit on her head, but still a kiss. I simply say no to keep my anger under control and explain a bit of how I am feeling. She assures me friends sometimes do things like that, and it means absolutely nothing romantic. For Mark's sake, it better not.

I get behind her in the lounging chair and pull her close. She pulls the blanket around the both of us, and we eventually drift off to sleep watching the stars together.

Chapter 26: Olive

"What do you mean he lied?"

"He told the old beast that you asked him to come to your room, and he was uncomfortable."

"I would say I can't believe this, but I do. People like him say whatever they can to make themselves look innocent and to stay out of trouble and near their victims. I will need to be more vigilant when he is near."

"I will as well. I will kill him if I must, Olive."

"Maybe the knife throwing scared him enough."

"I missed."

"Maybe that was for the best. I wouldn't want that on your conscience."

"You are too sweet, my Olive. I would happily kill for you."

"I don't want you to kill for me. I couldn't live with that on me."

"Olive, I will not let someone hurt you. I saw the intention in his eyes."

"Well, maybe try not to just jump to the kill first."

"I shall try for you." He says and kisses my head.

“I should tell you, I threw a wrench at the old man as well.”

“What? Why?”

“He said he could feel me and that I should behave in his house. HIS house. This is MY house. So, I threw it towards him and he walked out.”

“I can’t believe he can feel you, too! So those excuses he keeps making to me are just lies. So, are you going to visit his dreams too?” I tease.

“NO. You are the only human I want to know. You are different. You are mine.”

“Well, are you mine?” I questioned.

“Only yours.”

“Then I'm yours.” He kisses my head, and I feel his smile as he does.

“I remembered something today that may help in our search.”

“Oh, that's great! What is it?”

“I remembered someone with long grey hair, chanting, and a fire. Not a small fire. One like something substantial burning.”

“This is good. I will do some digging and see if there are any events I can come up with that may account for those events.”

"Thank you for trying to free me, Olive."

"You're welcome. I must admit I have my own selfish reasons for wanting you free."

"Oh, and what would those be?"

"I will get to see you anytime I want. I will be able to hear your voice without the recorder or being in our dreams. Plus, I get to show you off to the world." I say with a giggle.

"I want those things and so much more. I believe it will be I who will be showing you off to the world, though." I just smile and snuggle back into him.

I wake up around 2:00 a.m. because I got very cold, so we go to my room, well, I guess our room, honestly. I am still cold after I get in bed, so I get up and add a sweatshirt to my pajamas. I climb back into the bed and find my way back to him. I cuddle up to him and breathe him in. After a while, I drift off to sleep.

I wake back up in his arms, exactly where I want to be. I look up at him, and he is already looking at me with those black as night eyes. I could stare at him all night. His eyes searched mine with a question that he already knew the answer to.

He brushed the hair away from my face, behind my ear. His fingertips lingered on my cheeks softly, and then he leaned in. He was not fast or hungry but slow and with meaning and intention. When he kissed me fully, I melted against him. He kissed me warm and deep and maddeningly slow like he had nothing to do but to be tasting me, breathing me in. We break the kiss, and I begin to kiss down his strong jawline, down his neck slowly. I raise up to remove my sweatshirt and nightgown. His eyes are watching my every move. I pull his tunic up, and he removes it and his pants. I resume kissing and licking, slow, methodical, until I am dangerously close to taking him into my mouth.

He tilts my head toward him, "You do not have to do this."

I shake my head, "I want to."

My mouth finally claims him. I'm not sure if he will be able to fit, honestly. I take him in my mouth, hollowing my cheeks, sucking slowly at first, consuming, exploring, worshiping him. I brush my tongue over his sensitive skin, and he sucks in a breath and groans my name, which only feeds my enthusiasm. I looked up into his eyes, full of a mix of hunger, awe, and devotion. My mouth continues to move with confidence and desire. I want to unmake him not just for pleasure but to show him how deeply I want to give. With every flick of my tongue, he begins to come more undone. Every one of my strokes, sucks, and licks become more deliberate. He begins to buck beneath me, and I hum in approval.

His hands grab my hair, and he quickens his pace. I continue to hum and gag a bit when he hits the back of my throat, and that seems to add to his impending wave of pleasure. He comes with a roar, and I take all of him until he is trembling and breathless. I climb back up beside him and rest my head on his chest. He tilts my head and kisses me, "Your turn, my Olive." He begins trailing kisses down my neck. I stop him,

"I didn't do that so you would give it to me back. I just wanted to show you how much I want you and want you to feel good."

"I know this. I want to worship you, Olive. I want to taste you. I cannot get enough of you."

"If you really want to, but I would be satisfied if you just hold me for a while."

"No, Olive. You do not have to do something you do not want to do. You should tell me what you need and want. I will never make you do anything other than that."

"I just don't want to make you mad or make you leave me."

"I will never do that, Olive. You are stuck with me. I know others have made you feel this way, but I will never do that to you. I love you unconditionally."

"Thank you. I am new to this feeling and honestly, I'm not quite sure how to act."

"You never have to worry with me, my love. Please be yourself."

"Will you hold me?"

"Absolutely."

I lie back against his chest, where I can hear his steady heartbeat beneath my ear. His fingers are stroking small circles along my spine, absentmindedly and tenderly. The silence is full and rich with everything we have said and do not need to say.

Chapter 27: HIM

"This is a children's movie, Olive." I click play on the recorder.

"Oh, no, you don't. No movie shaming! I love Disney movies, and that is ok, mister!" I smile and chuckle at her bossy tone.

"Okay, okay, I surrender. Let us watch this Alice in Wonderland."

"That's better!" She says with a big smile that makes me melt.

I pull her close, and she leans into me. As the movie continues, I find myself watching her more than this creation that I must admit I do not enjoy. For her, I will endure it, though. My thoughts drift to thoughts of our future and what it could be. What can it be for someone like me who does not remember his past? Will I get my memories back? What if I am someone unworthy of her? What if she realizes this and leaves me? Would I be able to control myself when I meet her family? I do not believe I could. I would take them down where they stood for mistreating her and for allowing the abuse she has endured. I begin to get angry, and she senses it.

"Are you okay?"

"Yes."

"Um…You do realize I can feel the anger rolling off of you, right?"

"I am sorry, Olive, my thoughts drifted to unhappy things. I do not wish to speak of."

"I won't pressure you, but I am here if you would like to talk. You're not alone anymore, I'm here for you." With those sweet words, my mood eases, and I kiss her head.

"Thank you, my sweet Olive. Let us watch your children's movie." She elbows me and laughs.

"It's over but I will start another one you may like better."

"Oh, wonderful," I joke.

"Haha, keep it up and no kisses tonight!"

"I take it back; these movies are masterpieces."

"That's better." She says with a humph, a smile, then crosses her arms. She changes it to a movie called The Beauty and the Beast. "You will love this one! It's my favorite. I wanted to dress up as these characters, but I don't believe you would want Mark to be my love interest."

"No, I would not want that. Not at all."

We watch her movie, and I will admit this one is considerably better, although I could do without the talking household items. I see Olive and me as the beauty and the beast, so that makes it more enjoyable.

"When I am free, I will dress as this beast for you. Mark can be this Gaston character."

"Aww, really, you would? Also, Mark is not a Gaston," she says with a laugh.

"Yes, and fine, he can be the clock or candlestick." That sends her into a fit of giggles. I love it.

The movie ends, and as if her stomach senses that, it growls loudly. I realize that she has not eaten all day. I need to take better care of her.

"Olive, you have not eaten all day. This is not good."

"I just don't want to run into Grandmother or Steve."

"I will go and make sure they are not there first."

"That would be great. I'm sorry, I'm just trying not to make waves before the party."

"Do not be sorry. When I am free, I will take far from these people."

I go downstairs to look for the dusty old hag and the slimy friend. I check all around and see no signs of the two rats. I only find the old man asleep in his chair with the television on, some show about fixing up old houses. I go back and tell Olive that she can come down and do whatever she needs to do, and we head back down. On the way to the kitchen, she sees the old man, and she grabs a blanket and covers him with it. How does she have such kindness for those who do not care for her? That is one of the things that makes her unique among these pathetic humans. She makes her way to the kitchen, prepares her food, and grabs a snack and drink for later. As we head upstairs, we hear the front door close. We turn back, and the she devil stands in the foyer staring at Olive with a look of pure contempt, then smiles and heads towards the living room. Olive shakes her head and turns to go towards her room. I want to go down and scare that look off her face, but instead, I follow Olive. Call it self control or growth, but it goes against every instinct I have.

As Olive eats, she suggests we go ahead and research what we can on my new memories. So, we log on to her computer and get started once she finishes her meal.

"There are so many time periods it could be. Call it a hunch, but I believe the evidence is pointing to the French and Indian War. There were tribes on both the British and French sides. Right now, I'm not sure which you were on."

"I will try to access more memories. I cannot help but feel weak because I cannot recall what I need to, and it makes me furious."

"That's totally okay, I would feel the same way if I were in your position. We will figure this out, I promise," she says and smiles. I kiss her head and prop my chin on top while I hold her close.

Chapter 28: Olive

This weekend with him was so relaxing. We watched movies in bed, tangled up with each other. Slept, still tangled up together. I do not know the last time, if ever, I have felt like this with someone, safe, loved, valued, beautiful, cherished. He is so strong but gentle with me, protective even if it's a little murderous sometimes. He is honest and loyal, and he can be a bit assertive, but I don't really mind, because in certain situations, that is a big turn on. The best part of my day is when I get home to him. No more do I enter to that heavy, angry presence every day like when we first moved in. Now he is calm when I come in and is always finding ways to touch me, even though I can't see him. Next month can't get here quick enough. I have to find a way to free him.

I have effectively avoided Grandmother this week. After the look she gave me Saturday, I thought she would seek me out and find ways to put me down, but she didn't, and I didn't seek her out either. I know she was upset about Steve being upstairs with me, but how so? I say, "*Steve is lying, my not ghost boyfriend heard him tell you, his lies. Here is what really happened.*" She wouldn't believe me even if that sounded sane. It is Thursday night, so only two more days to dodge her; that's totally doable. I walk in the door, happy that no one but Granddad is around.

"Hi Granddad, did you have a good day?"

“It was fine, just gave your grandmother her meds, so I am ready for my nightly shows.”

“Well, I will let you get to it. Goodnight.”

I go upstairs, and he is there waiting. We head to our room. I hear a spitting sound from my bathroom, and the door is cracked. I tiptoe over and see Grandmother spitting her meds into the toilet. Just as I go to step back, she turns her head and sees me. I try to hurry to my room, but she pulls me back by my hair.

“What do you think you’re doing, spying on me? Whatever you thought you saw, you didn’t. Do you understand me, you fucking fat ass?” She hisses into my ear with my hair tightly wrapped in her hand.

“I didn’t see anything. I swear.”

“First, you think you can have Steve and now…” She is cut off, and we both are thrown to the floor, and she releases her hold on my hair. I scramble away, and I feel him between us.

“You will pay for that, you bitch, and all the trouble you have caused me through the years.”

“Why Grandmother? I thought you were better? I thought we were doing better?”

“Ha! I have been faking it, Ollie. Steve doesn't like it when I treat you poorly, plus I like the attention I get if I seem fragile. See win win. Except I have had to tolerate you.”

"What about the party?"

"Oh, we are having it. A Halloween party will be great for my business. So, it's legit." She doubles over as she has been kicked, and I run to my room and lock the door.

After a few minutes, I hear her go down the hall and then down the stairs. He finally comes in and wraps me in his arms. I am honestly not surprised by her actions or words. I feel so hollow, so void of feeling right now. I have no tears left to cry for her. I lean into him and breathe in his earthy, woodsy scent. "Can we go ahead and go to sleep?" I ask. He slides his hand into mine and gives it a slight squeeze. I slip to the bathroom under his guard and wash my face and brush my teeth. We go back to our room and lock the door. I climb into bed, and he wraps his arms around me; it doesn't take long for sleep to claim me.

"Would you like to talk about it?"

"There isn't anything really to talk about. She hasn't changed. We both suspected it. It just fits her past patterns. I guess I was stupid to hope it was different this time."

"No, you are not stupid, Olive. You want a family that you see others have, and unfortunately, the family you have cannot see how extraordinary you are. They are hung up on things from their past that have nothing to do with you, but they take it out on you. That is unacceptable. You deserve better. I will give you better, my Olive. You are my family now, and hopefully, when I am free, we can build our own family."

"Honestly, I have always wanted a family but never really thought it would happen for me. I mean, I have been beaten down my whole life. What if I pass my hang ups down to my children? Anyway, who would ever want a family with me?"

"Olive, I want a family with you. Any man would be lucky to have such a woman. Of course, I would have to dispose of him and take his place because you are mine."

"What if you are freed and see that there are better people out there? What if I am not enough anymore?" I lower my head, bracing for rejection. He tilts my chin up.

"Olive, this will not happen. I have seen many humans before you. None of them were you. None will ever be you. You were sent for me, and I for you. I believe this. I want you. I love you. Forever." He kisses me then. A soft, loving kiss meaningful like he is saying, "*I'm here. I care. I see you.*" A caress in kiss form that makes everything else fade away.

The next morning, I successfully sneak out before anyone notices. I call Mark and see if he wants to meet up at the local coffee shop, Sip Happens, for coffee and breakfast.

"Ok, tell me what is going on. You are never up and out this early," he says suspiciously. I fill him in on what happened last night, and to say he is livid would be an understatement.

“I’m going over there right now! No one is going to treat you that way, Olive.”

“It's over. I just needed to vent.”

“What about your party tomorrow?”

“What about it?”

“I don’t think it’s a good idea to go. Let’s go out and do something else. Anything else?”

“I have to go. It's my party. It will be the last thing I do with them. I swear. Plus, I already invited everyone from work. It would be embarrassing to uninvite them.”

“Olive, I don’t like this, but I will be there for you no matter what.” He puts his hand over mine.

“Thank you, Mark. Not just for this, but for being so good to me.”

“Olive, you are one of the most caring, intelligent, accepting people I know. Of course I’m here for you, beautiful.” He raises my hand, kisses it, and smiles. I smile back. I am so glad I have him in my life.

“What did I ever do to deserve you?”

“Just lucky, I guess. Now, let’s head to work.”

When we got in and started working, Jennifer came by and invited us to a haunted house tonight. She told us to dress up but in something different than our party costumes. So, Mark and I decided to scavenge the stores after work to see what we can find. We are able to find a goddess costume that is a bit more revealing than I am typically comfortable with. But, hey, it's ok on Halloween, right? Mark found a leather gladiator costume to go with mine, and after spending a small fortune, we are set to go out with our friends. Mark suggests that we go change at his house and head out from there. While I hate not being able to let HIM know what I am doing, I can't really explain that to Mark, so I agree.

Mark shows me to his guest room to get changed. This costume seemed like it covered more in the store. Holy shit. Okay. I can do this. I'm a bad bitch, right? I look in the mirror and honestly, I feel like a goddess. I might wear this outfit every day. Seriously, I am *feeling* myself! It is a gunmetal colored bodysuit with a plunging V cut lace up front. Attached is a glittering black veil like fabric that has very high cuts to reveal my legs and glittery silver thigh straps. I touch it off with a pair of platform silver heels I grabbed while we were out. I step out into the living room where Mark is waiting.

"Fuck, Olive." He says, walking toward me.

"Is that good?" I ask meekly.

"Yes, Olive, it is good. You look ethereal." He takes the black spiked crown from my hand, places it on my head, and fingers through my hair, adjusting it just so. He turns me to the mirror, "See, Olive. You are perfect."

"You don't look so bad yourself. That looks like it was made for you." I say, trying to get the focus off of me.

"Oh, this old thing," he jokes. He seriously does look handsome; he always does, but tonight is different. His sleeveless leather suit has a deep V in the front, accentuating his chest and shoulders; the material clings to him, highlighting exactly how muscular he is. The wrist cuffs and black boots complete the look, and he looks straight out of a gladiator movie.

"Seriously, you're going to get so many looks tonight."

"As long as I am with you, I don't care. It's you and me tonight," he says with a wink.

"I believe I'm cramping your style every weekend; you have hardly had any new date stories to tell." We both laugh.

"There is no one I would rather be spending time with than you. Now let's go before the others start wondering where we are."

We pull up to the Acres of Abyss Haunted Experience and find Candy and Jennifer. Candy is dressed as a sexy Ghostbuster, and Jennifer is a sexy clown. I shake my head and laugh in my head; those two fashionistas definitely go all in on Halloween, and I love it. There are these huge bonfires at the center of the event, so we head over and find seats to warm up.

"Damn, Olive, you look hot as hell!" Candy says.

"For real, girl! You too, Mark, but Olive, your costume looks gorgeous on you." Jennifer adds.

"Thanks, I think? I agree about Olive, though, isn't she beautiful?" says Mark.

"Thank you, guys. It's out of my comfort zone, but I must say I do feel confident."

"Don't look, but there is a guy in that group behind us checking you out, Olive," Candy says.

"I'm sure he isn't looking at me."

"Oh, he's coming over!" Candy says excitedly. Mark slides his arm around my waist, and the man turns and goes back to his group.

"Mark! You totally just cockblocked her!" Jennifer exclaims.

"She doesn't want some random guy hitting on her while she is out with us," he replies.

"What! Maybe she does!" Jennifer says. Everyone looks at me.

“I would rather focus on my time with you guys. Thank you, Mark. Before we go, let's do the haunted hayride.”

“Yes, I love those things!” Jennifer exclaimed

We walk over to the line, and Mark keeps his hand on the small of my back the whole time we wait. It doesn't make me feel uncomfortable; it makes me feel like he is looking out for me. He knows I want to focus on having fun with my friends, and large groups often make me nervous. The guy from earlier probably meant no harm, but in the back of my mind, I can’t help but think what if his friends put him up to approaching me as a joke. As if he senses my sudden wave of self consciousness Mark takes my hand and gives it a squeeze. I love that he knows me so well. It is finally our turn. As we ride, men in masks jump at us and the girls, and I joke about how we would let them chase us through the woods. Mark rolls his eyes. Before the ride ends, a man in a clown costume jumps at us.

“AAAAHH!! I KNEW THERE WOULD BE A CLOWN! I HATE CLOWNS!” Jennifer screams at the top of her lungs.

“You are ok, deep breaths,” Candy says to her, rubbing her arm.

“Jenn, you are literally dressed as a clown!” Mark jokes.

"Yeah, but in her defense, she can't see herself dressed up." I retort.

"You guys are jerks! Accurate, but still jerks." Jennifer says with a laugh.

We exit the ride and spot the guy from earlier, and Mark slips his hand in mine again as we walk by him. My mind drifts to HIM, and I feel so guilty for not going by the house to let him know I would be out late. He is trapped there, and I am just out here having fun. I can't imagine what he might be thinking right now. I take that back. I do know, and that has me feeling even guiltier. I slide on my long coat, Mark has been carrying for me, and we head to the parking lot and say our goodbyes. Mark and I get in his car and start the drive back to his house.

"You okay, Olive? I hope I didn't overstep back there. I was just trying to protect you."

"Oh, you were totally fine. You knew I just wanted to be there with you guys, having fun."

"So, what's on your mind?"

"I guess I'm worried about tomorrow and what stunt Grandmother will try to pull."

"I know, but hey, any signs of her trying anything and we are out of there. Okay?"

"Thanks, Mark. Seriously, I don't know what I would do without you."

"Hey, it's late, why don't you stay the night?"

"I wish I could. I really do need to get home, though. I am supposed to help decorate tomorrow."

"For your own party?"

"Apparently, it's all hands on deck." I shrug.

"Okay, but I am coming over early and bringing you breakfast. AND helping you all day."

"That sounds perfect. Thank you, Mark."

We pull into his driveway, and as I go to get in my car, he pulls me back into a hug and kisses my cheek. "Thank you for everything you do and are, Olive."

He smiles, and I return with one of my own. "Back at you. See you in the morning." I turn and get into my car.

It's 2:00 in the morning before I get home, and when I walk in the door, I feel him heavily. He isn't near me, but I feel his anger and unease everywhere. I see Granddad as I walk by the living room.

"It has been this way all evening."

"Like what?" I play dumb.

"Heavy, oppressive. Whatever you do to calm whatever is here, please do it so I can get some rest."

"I will try, Granddad."

“That’s my girl. Goodnight.” He gets up from his chair and heads to his room.

His presence is so consuming that it is difficult to figure out exactly where he is. I find him on the back deck, which is an odd spot for him to be. It feels like he is pacing. I knew he was strong, but tonight he feels more powerful than he ever has.

“I’m so sorry. I didn’t realize I would be out so late. I need to find a way to communicate with you better. I know you had to be worried, and I am so sorry.”

I feel him calm a bit and place his hand on my face. “Let’s go to our room. I really want to see you. I have missed you so much.” We move quietly through the house and up the stairs. Once in our room, I lock the door and take my coat off, dropping it to the floor. I feel him still, and I hear the click of the recorder.

“Olive, what are you wearing?” his voice deep and rough.

“It's a costume I wore to a haunted house my friends and I went to tonight. Do you like it?” I ask as I move my hands over my breast and waist, teasing him. His hands replace mine.

“I do not like others have seen what is mine, but you are divine, my Olive. You are a goddess, and I shall worship you tonight.” I feel his kisses starting to trail from my neck down my chest.

“Let’s go to bed. I want to see you.” I say heavily, as I let my outfit fall to the floor.

I don’t even fully open my eyes, and he is on me. His hands are trailing down to my thighs with reverence, like he is memorizing the shape of me. His lips brush over sensitive skin as if he is savoring every moment exploring me, worshipping me. I gasp as he settles between my legs, every one of my nerves waking under the heat of his breath. He looks up at me once, eyes full of that hunger I have seen in them before. Then he dips down again, and I forget how to breathe. The way he moves his mouth, he knows exactly how to unmake me. I arch against him. My fingers thread in his silky, black hair, grounding myself in the way he makes me feel. Undone. Cherished. Completely seen. When the waves of pleasure finally hit, it’s like being broken and remade all at once. I am left a shaking and panting mess.

Chapter 29: HIM

All evening, my head was clouded with the worst of thoughts when Olive did not come home. Was there an accident? Is she somewhere in need of help, and I cannot get to her? Did she finally decide to leave? Did she figure out she loves Mark? Am I not enough, and she decided I am not worth the hassle of dealing with me anymore?

When I saw her and she apologized, some of the worry eased. When she let her coat drop to the floor, I lost all thoughts I had. She is truly a goddess and deserves to be worshipped, and I will be the only one to do so.

She is so beautiful like this. Skin flushed, lips parted, and eyes glazed with the kind of pleasure that makes a man feel like a god. I stay on my knees for a moment longer to watch her body tremble in the aftershocks of what I have just done to her. Although something roared inside of me with pride, that is not why I watch her. I am in awe. Like I have just touched fire and lived to feel the burn. I still taste her on my tongue when I rise over her, letting myself press into her slowly and heavily. I gather her into my arms, needing contact with her skin with nothing between us. Neither of us spoke, but every breath, every heartbeat, spoke for us. We belong to each other. I kiss her unhurriedly. Not to ignite passion, but to further worship her.

We lie there in comfortable quiet, tangled together. Content, almost complete. Nothing will be complete until I am free of this curse, though. I know Olive will help figure this out. I need to help her by remembering more. Never have I had to before, so I am not sure what to do or how to even begin. So, I focus on what I already know. Long grey hair, red coats, symbols, fire. No, not just fire. Burning structures, like an encampment. It must have been a British encampment on fire. I get another flash: an older, grey haired male in the middle of camp chanting with those symbols around him. Did he set the fire? Did I?

"You seem lost in thought."

"I am sorry. I had another memory."

"Really? What is it?"

"It was a British soldier encampment on fire, and an older male with long, grey hair in the middle of the chaos. He was chanting, with the symbols drawn in the dirt around him."

"Oh wow. That sounds like some kind of battle. I will see what I can find on it when we wake up."

"No. It is your birthday, Olive. It can wait until later."

"While we are talking about my birthday, Mark is bringing me breakfast in the morning and helping set everything up for the party."

I get up from the bed and begin to pace in front of it.

"While I am really enjoying this view, don't be upset. I promise that there is nothing between Mark and me. He is not my type anyway."

"Oh, really? What is your type, Olive?" I ask as I crawl on the bed toward her.

"Tall, tanned, shadowy black hair, deep onyx eyes, deep husky voice…broody."

"I am not broody." I start kissing her neck.

"You're a little broody." She distracts me and begins trailing kisses across my collarbone.

"You win, my goddess," I say as we fall back into the bed, tangling into one another once again.

Chapter 30: Olive

I wake up snuggled up to him with his arm wrapped around me, mindlessly stroking my arm.

"As much as I hate to, I have to get up and get dressed before Mark gets here." He pulls me closer, "Or he can come in and see me naked." He releases me, and I laugh.

I get my shower and head back to the room in a pair of jeans and a sweatshirt. He already made the bed for me. "Thank you! That is really sweet!"

I hear the click of the recorder. "Do not tell anyone ever that I am *sweet*," he says, amused.

"Oh, when you're free, I'm going to tell everyone how sweet you are," I say, laughing. Suddenly, he is there, hugging me from behind, kissing my neck. I love these playful times with him.

"OLLIE! YOUR FRIEND IS HERE!" Grandmother screams from the foyer. He reluctantly lets go and I go out to greet Mark. By the time I get to him, Grandmother is chatting away. He is looking very uninterested.

"Happy Birthday, Olive!" Marks interrupts her. He grabs me into a hug.

"Well, I will leave you two. See you later, Mark." Grandmother says effectively, avoiding wishing me a happy birthday.

Mark and I go upstairs to my room. When we get to my room, it feels heavier, and I know HE is unhappy with Mark being in our space.

"I got your favorite breakfast: eggs Benedict and fruit with fresh orange juice from The Early Bird Cafe."

"OMG! YAY! Thank you so much! You're the best!" I say and immediately feel HIM at my side. If Mark weren't looking, I would roll my eyes at the possessiveness happening right now.

"I wanted to make sure your day started off great. Which brings me to my next surprise…" he pulls out a small box from his coat pocket.

"Mark, you didn't have to get me a gift."

"I wanted to. I wanted you to feel as special as you are, Olive." He gives me the box, and I open it to find an olive leaf vine necklace I saw at Tiffany's one day while we were in the city shopping.

"Mark, this is too much. How did you remember? OMG. Thank you so much! I love it!!"

"Olive, you deserve the best. I remember it because it was something you loved."

Before I thought about who else was in the room, I gave Mark a huge hug, and he kissed my cheek. The air in the room went cold.

"Is your room always drafty like this?" Mark asks with a shiver.

"Sometimes. It's an old house." I say as I put on my necklace.

"It looks beautiful on you, Olive. Now, eat before it gets cold. Well, colder."

We sit on the bed, eat breakfast, watch TV, and chat. All the while, HE sulks in the corner, creating a thick, heavy air about the room. Although I do get it, it has to be incredibly difficult to watch your girlfriend spend time and get gifts from her male friend. Mark excuses himself to the bathroom, and I use the moment to address HIM.

"I'm sorry you feel left out. I cannot wait until we free you from this and you can be with me." The heaviness lightens, and I feel him caress my cheek. Mark comes back, and the touch is gone. I immediately miss it.

"I saw your sorry excuse for a grandmother down the hall and asked if we needed to help set up. She said her friends were helping her, so we are free to hang out all afternoon."

"Phew. I was not looking forward to spending time with her and Steve."

“After that big breakfast, I could go for a nap. What do you say?”

“I’m in!” I immediately regret it because I then realize HE will see me in the same bed as Mark. Well, it's not like we will be touching. We lie down facing the opposite way, and I almost instantly fall asleep.

“You allowed him to sleep in our bed.” HE says grumpily.

“How are you here? We aren’t touching?”

“I am touching you from beside OUR bed since that male is in OUR bed, Olive.”

“I’m sorry. I really am. I said okay without thinking about how it would make you feel. I know it is an innocent nap, but I didn’t think of you, and I am sorry.” I say, taking his face in my hands.

“This is not easy to see, my Olive.”

“I will wake up and move. I don't want you to have any doubt about how I feel for you.”

“No, stay here with me a little longer.” He puts his forehead to mine.

“I love you, my not ghost”

“I love you, my Olive.”

Movement in the bed rouses me from my sleep. Mark is up and looking at my bookshelves. “Sorry, I didn't mean to wake you. I just thought I would check out your books."

"You probably won't find anything you'll like over there."

"Oh, I recognize this from social media, you naughty thing." He says with a laugh.

"Oh shit, Mark! We need to get dressed! The others will be here soon!" I exclaim as I jump out of the bed after I look at my phone and see what time it is.

He heads to the bathroom to change, while I change in my room. I forgot how short this dress is. HE may not let me leave this room. While typically I would be fine with that, tonight I am needed downstairs with my friends. I slide on my powdery, blue dress with the lace up, fitted bodice and sweetheart neckline. I add my white, ruffled petticoat underneath and pull up my thigh high tights. I will need Mark to help with my shoes because I can't see the buckles of my black Mary Janes over my underskirt. He knocks and I open the door for him. He looks like a handsome Mad Hatter in his costume. He took the idea of the character and turned him more adult like with a Victorian three piece suit and a hat. He did well…very well.

"Could you help me buckle my shoes?"

"Absolutely. You look beautiful, Olive."

He buckles my shoe and adjusts my tights. As he does, we hear a low growl.

"Olive, did you hear that?"

"It was probably from the start of the party."

"Maybe, but it sounded like it came from in here."

"I don't know. I didn't hear it that well." I lie. I heard and know exactly where it came from.

"Oh well. I guess we'd better head down." He finally says.

We arrive downstairs, and honestly, things look great. As you walk in from the front door, there are black velvet drapes hanging at the entrance to the living room and again at the entrance to the stairs. All of the lights are dim, and there are fake candles in elegant, black candelabras everywhere. There is a fog machine that is creating a light mist across the floor and haunting music playing. I must admit, Grandmother did a great job. I am honestly shocked.

We go outside to wait for Candy and Jennifer to arrive and notice that even the front lawn is decorated. Black fairy lights, moss, and bones are scattered around with black and silver painted pumpkins. Mark and I look at each other, surprised.

"It's about time you showed up to the party, Ollie. Come stand out here and greet the guests," Grandmother orders.

"Who are all these people? I thought this was my birthday party."

"Yes, and an opportunity for me to impress important clients. Just smile and greet, Ollie. It is really that simple," she spins and walks away with a smug strut.

"I'm going after her and letting her have it," Mark says as she walks away.

"No. When the others get here, we will abandon post and enjoy the party." I say.

"Have you thought about living with me anymore, Olive? I don't mean to be pushy, but I don't like the idea of you being here with her."

"I have, and honestly, I want to, but there is something keeping me here just a little longer. I can't explain it."

We greet several people I don't know, a lot of my family and family friends, and of course, Steve. Finally, Candy and Jennifer arrive.

"OMG, Olive, you look amazing!! That is your color!! Happy Birthday!!!!" Candy says excitedly.

"Olive, you seriously look great! Oh, and Mark, you look fine too. Happy Birthday, Olive!!" Jennifer follows and gives me a hug.

"You both look amazing yourselves! Now, let's go have some fun!" I say.

We go inside and enjoy a light snack at the food table. I feel my grandmother walk up before I see her.

"Oh, Ollie, be careful. You will pop those laces right out." She laughs cruelly and walks away.

"Excuse me, you can't talk to her that way." Mark scolds.

"Oh, it is just a joke Ollie and I have. Right, Ollie?" she replies with a wave of her hand dismissing Mark.

"Well, it isn't funny. You need to stop." Mark says. Grandmother puts her nose in the air and walks away.

"Thank you, Mark."

"What the heck was that?" Candy asks.

"My grandmother."

"She needs an attitude adjustment, and I will be happy to give her one," Jennifer says, grabbing a gin bottle.

"No, it's fine. I'm used to it." I say with a weak laugh.

"It is not okay, but I will respect your wishes…for now," Jennifer says, putting the bottle down.

Suddenly, we hear a commotion in the living room and rush to investigate.

Apparently, Grandmother fell. Well, I should say she was pushed, because HE is quickly beside me.

"It's ok, everyone, I have damage from when I had polio as a child. This happens sometimes," she says, and everyone fawns over her. It's just like her to milk the moment and get as much attention as she can.

Mark looks at me, and I shake my head. "Nope, never happened, and no, she doesn't fall frequently." He just shakes his head and turns to lead us back towards the kitchen.

After a while, the music turns into dance music, and we all make our way to the makeshift dance floor in the living room. We are dancing and having fun when I catch my grandmother and a couple of her friends are giggling. It is obvious it is at me. Mark must notice too because he starts to put his hands on my waist and gets close.

He whispers in my ear, "Is this okay?" I nod and we continue to dance.

Evidently, the show worked because they stopped laughing at me and all had sour looks on their faces. I feel HIS heaviness and anger leave the room, and I know I have messed up. The song ends, and I excuse myself to go upstairs to my bathroom. Really, I am going to HIM.

I reach the top of the stairs, and Steve is there. Unease prickles the back of my neck, but I ignore it and try to pass him. I say hello, and as I pass by, he grabs my wrist. Panic runs through my veins, and I try to pull from his grip.

"Olive, there's no need to be scared. I want to make you feel good."

"Steve, don't do this. Please let me go."

"Why would I do that? I have put up with that stupid grandmother of yours to get to you for months now. It's time to claim my prize."

"Steve, please let me go." I cry because he has both wrists now and is pushing me into the wall.

"I can't do that, Olive." He says, letting go of one wrist to open the guest room door. I take the opportunity to break his hold and run. He grabs my hair, and I let out a yelp as he pulls me back, and I hit the wall. The music covers any noise that we might make. I feel his hot, sticky breath on my neck, and he rips my dress. I free a hand and scratch his face. He slams my head into the wall, and I hit the floor. The next thing I know, Steve is in the air, and I can see HIM holding him there. Everything happens so fast after that. I hear the snap of Steve's neck, and HE tosses Steve down the stairs. HE bends down to me, taking my face in his hands, and begins to flicker out, when we hear Mark from the bottom of the stairs.

"Olive, what the fuck just happened?" HE flickers out, but Mark definitely saw HIM.

Mark rushes up the stairs to me and checks me over. He says something about bruising on my arms, and my head is bleeding, but I am in a state of shock, and it doesn't really register with me.

"Olive, I saw him attack you. You scratched him, and he backed up and fell. Okay? Do you hear me, Olive?"

"Yes."

"Repeat it to me, Olive. Come on, sweet girl."

"He attacked me. I scratched him. He backed up too far and fell."

"That's my girl. I'm calling the ambulance, and I will be right back."

I'm sitting against the wall with my arms wrapped around my knees and HIM beside me, holding me. I can hear the commotion below. Grandmother screaming. Paramedics are coming in. Police are entering the house. Mark brings a paramedic and an officer up to me.

"Olive, can the paramedics check you out? Then the police officer would like to ask you a few questions. Okay, my sweet girl?" Mark speaks to me, and I look at him and nod, unable to speak yet. After looking me over, the paramedic thinks that I should go to the hospital overnight to be monitored because of my head injury. The officer says that they would meet us there and ask me questions at the hospital, where I would be more comfortable. All I can do is numbly nod my head to them. HE has my hand as they put me on the gurney and take me downstairs. HE doesn't let go until he is forced out of the way. I feel him behind us the whole way down, though. Him and all the anger and sadness he is carrying with him.

We reach the bottom of the stairs, and they have already moved Steve's body from the house. I hear Grandmother wailing from outside when we get to the front door.

Mark catches up to us after he went to grab a change of clothes for me from my room.

"Ignore her, Olive. I'm with you. I have you, baby girl." Mark comforts me.

"YOU! YOU WHORE! THIS IS ALL YOUR FAULT!! YOU KILLED HIM!!" Grandmother screams.

"No. No, I didn't. I swear. He attacked me. He tried to…" I choke down a sob.

"You liar! You never liked him, and he was so nice to you! I read your journals, and you always hated him. You probably did this on purpose!" She continues to rant.

"Ma'am, you need to settle down or go inside your residence." An officer tells her.

"Oh, I'm sorry. I am just so distraught!" she cries.

"Don't worry about her. I have you. You're going to be okay, Olive." Mark reassures me.

I feel HIM beside me before they put me in the ambulance. He kisses my head and then my hand as they load me up. When will I be with him again? Will I be with him again? I can't stand the thought of not being with him. I push those thoughts out of my head for now. I need to focus on this.

"Where is Mark? Is he not coming with us?" I ask the paramedic as I start to panic.

"He is driving to the hospital to be with you. He will meet us there," he says. He closes the doors to the ambulance, and we leave.

Chapter 31: HIM

All day, I have had to endure this Mark with MY Olive. Now he has his hands on her where my hands should be, his mouth so close to her neck where I should be kissing her. He is whispering so close to her ear and making her smile. I cannot take it anymore. I must leave this space before I lose myself. I go upstairs to our room to try to calm down. I slam the door and begin to pace. She says she and Mark are just friends. Friends do not act this way, even I know this. Does she think I cannot see this? That I am stupid? Does she not care for me as she says she does? Does she not love me?

I sit on the bed, head in my hands. Perhaps she would be better with Mark. He can give her what I cannot. I am stuck here with no release in sight, cursed to be tied here, long forgotten by everyone. No, not by everyone. Olive knows me. Olive loves me. She is MINE. He cannot have her. We chose each other, and he will not threaten our future together. I stand and go to claim my woman.

As I get to the end of the hall, I see Steve and Olive. He has his filthy hands on her. ON HER. ON MY WOMAN. Rage consumes me. I do not think. I only act. I grab him away from her. His eyes bulge as I grip his throat as tightly as I can, reveling in the way he struggles beneath my hand. He looks me in the eyes. He can see me. Good. I want him to see me when I end him for touching what is mine. I flick my wrist, and his neck breaks. I toss him down the stairs like the insignificant garbage he is…*was* and kneel down to check on Olive. She can see me, too. I take her face into my hands, and I feel myself getting weaker. Before I fade completely, I hear Mark take in a breath at the sight of me.

Olive is in a state of shock. She is not speaking. I sit and hold her, waiting for medical assistance for her head injury and the bruising on her arms. Mark brings help and stays beside her as well. I do not like this, but this is what she needs, so I allow it. Mark gathers some things for her from our room for the hospital stay tonight. I stay with her until the absolute last second, I can, and as the doors to the ambulance close, I hear her ask for Mark. It is like a knife to the chest to hear her call for him.

I stand numbly in the front yard as the guests and officers leave one by one. She asked for Mark. She wanted Mark. No. This is not about me. She needs someone there to comfort her, and I cannot be there. He is just a friend and will be there when she needs him. That is what is important. Whatever Olive needs is what matters and nothing else.

I walk back to the house, and as I go inside, I hear the cries of the hideous old hag. She is sad over that disgusting piece of shit and is blaming Olive.

"I read her journals. She has been planning something. All she kept saying was that he was creepy and made her uncomfortable. When in reality, he was just ignoring and denying her advances. Apparently, she has a secret boyfriend, too, whom she is so in love with. Poor Mark, such a sweet, trusting boy. How does such a horrible cow like that get these men?"

All of the little hag women friends nod their heads, and like always, the old man is silent. Anger is burning like fire in my chest, and before I add to my body count tonight, I go upstairs to our room. I make sure the door is locked so that the revolting beast cannot get to my Olive's things. I lie on the bed and stare at the ceiling, feeling weakened from so much use of my power tonight. I was able to protect her, though. I wish I could be with her now. When she returns home, we will double down on our efforts to break this curse. I need to be with her. I have never tried to use sleep to stir memories, but now would be as good of a time as any. So, I lie here on the bed until sleep comes.

I am nowhere. I am in darkness. I am called a name I cannot hear. Over and over. There is chanting calling me forward, pulling me toward them. I feel the call, and I want to go. Suddenly, I am at the outskirts of a village. There is a male with long, grey hair. He smiles.

I wake up. Damn it. I want more, need more. I want to help provide Olive with as much information as possible. I take out paper and quickly write what I dreamt for her. I have an idea. I cannot always be with her right now, but my words can. I write her a letter and put it in her work bag. A little surprise to make her smile. What I would not do to have her here and smiling for me now.

It is morning now, so I go downstairs to wait for Olive to return home. The gremlin friends are back, helping their leader clean up from the party. She is still crying over the piece of garbage, Steve, and how she knows Olive did this on purpose, even if the police believe Olive's story. I am getting ready to walk away when she says that Olive is no longer welcome to live here. The earth seems to crumble beneath my feet. I cannot breathe. I feel physically ill. The world is spinning. She continues to speak about how evil Olive is and how she is just like her mother. She continues on until I cannot take any more and explode with a burst of energy, knocking her and her friends to the ground and shattering the mirrors and glass in the room. They are all stunned at first, and then the screams begin. I cannot enjoy it, though. I am going to lose my Olive because of this bitch. I go to her, and as I reach to grab her, Olive crosses my mind. I know she would not want this, even after everything. So, I back away. I allow all my anger to roll off of me so that these cruel, stupid women can all drown in it. One of the women says something about a priest, and I laugh. It wouldn't be my first run in with a member of the clergy in all my years here. Shit, maybe they will find a way to unbind me, and I can be free. The old man walks in and asks what happened. When the women try to explain, he shakes his head and turns around, going back to the garage.

I go to leave the room right as there is a knock at the door. It is an officer, Mark, and my Olive.

Chapter 32: Olive

I am finally at the hospital, and as promised, Mark is here with me. He let Candy and Jennifer know what was happening, and they are in the waiting room right now. The doctor has checked me out, and I have a concussion, a cut on the back of my head, and my arms are bruised up. Other than that, I will be fine. Physically anyway. They are going to keep me overnight for observation since I hit my head really hard. The police have taken pictures of my injuries and asked Mark and me questions about what happened with Steve tonight.

"That is all for now, Miss. If we need anything else, we will get in touch with you. Call us tomorrow, and we will go to the house while you gather your things," the officer tells me.

"Thank you, officer. I will give you a call before we head over there." I reply before he leaves.

"Candy and Jennifer would like to see you, but if it is too much tonight, I can have them wait until tomorrow." Marks says.

"No, they can come in tonight. We all have had a traumatic night."

"Olive, YOU have had a traumatic night. Don't you worry about us. We are fine."

"Maybe they can come in for just a little bit then?"

"I will go get them." He walks out to retrieve them from the waiting room.

"OH, Olive babes. I love you so much! We just wanted to check on you before we headed home." Candy says as she walks in the door.

"I knew I needed that gin bottle," Jennifer says, breaking the tension and making me smile.

"Okay, guys, you saw her. Now she needs rest. So, visiting time is over." Mark announces.

"Geez, possessive much, Mark? We will see you later, Olive. We love you." Jennifer says as they walk out.

"I'm okay, really."

"We both know that's not true, but I will not push you to talk about it. Soon, we *will* talk about the man I saw, though."

So, he did see HIM.

"We definitely can. Maybe not tonight, though. Please?"

"Not tonight. You need rest, my sweet girl."

"Will you stay with me?"

"As if you could get me to leave your side. Now try to get some sleep. I'm right here."

Tears slide down my face as I lie here trying to find sleep. I should be with HIM right now. I am not sad at what happened to Steve because if he tried to do that to me, he has or would have done that to someone else. I know what this means, though. I will not be able to return to HIM now. No more lazy movie days. No more long talks. No more staring at the stars together. No more anything together. It's over. I feel physically ill. I jump up from the bed, make my way to the bathroom, and am sick. Mark rushes to my side and holds my hair back. I crumple to the floor, sobbing, and he says nothing as he holds me and rubs my back. It is exactly what I need right now. Just not *who* I need. After a little bit, Mark helps me up. I brush my teeth and wash my face before climbing back in bed. The nurses bring Mark in a pullout chair to sleep in for the night, so he sets it up and holds my hand until finally sleep comes.

I dream of HIM. We are outside in a field. He is staring at the stars, just as we often do together. But this time, he is just out of reach. He can't hear me calling for him, calling a name I can't quite make out. Then Steve is grabbing me, pulling me back. His sticky, smelly breath is on my neck. Then, the sound of bone snapping. I jolt upward, waking Mark as I do. He had fallen asleep, holding my hand beside me.

"Are you okay, Olive?"

"Yeah. Just a bad dream. I'm sorry I woke you."

"Don't apologize, Olive. You have just been through something traumatic. You can wake me up anytime you need."

"I hate to ask this, but do you think I could take you up on your offer to stay with you for a little while. Just until I get my own place, of course."

"Olive, you didn't even need to ask. I already planned for you to come home with me today. You can stay as long as you want."

"Thank you, Mark. I don't know what I would do without you." I say, tearing up.

"You will never have to guess. You're stuck with me, sweet girl." He kisses my hand.

We both doze back off and I don't have another dream like before. I still dream of HIM. Though it is more like replaying memories. The nurse brings us both some breakfast and wakes us to let us know that I will be discharged by lunch. We eat, and I change into the sweatshirt and jeans Mark had grabbed me last night. Mark calls the officer we had last night and sets up a time to meet at my grandparents' house.

"I know you do not want to talk about it right now, but before I let you go to your room alone, will the person I saw last night hurt you?"

"No, he won't," I say in almost a whisper.

We pull up to the house in the truck that Mark rented, and of course, Grandmother and her friends are here. The crime scene tape is still up, and if you didn't know what happened here last night, it would look like any other decorated yard. Mark opens my car door and takes my hand as I step out. The officer greets us, and we make our way to the front door. Grandmother answers with her face red and blotchy from crying over Steve. HE immediately is at my side, holding my other hand.

"She is not allowed in here EVER again." She yells and goes to close the door.

"Ma'am, technically, she is allowed here. You have to give her 30 days' notice of eviction. Olive has decided to go ahead and gather her things today. I am here to make sure that it goes smoothly. If you could please stay on this side of the house until they have removed her belongings."

"Yes, sir, officer. I meant no disrespect. I am just so distraught over my friend's death and the circumstances in which he passed."

"Ma'am, if you could stay out of the foyer while they move her things." He is having none of her nonsense. Finally, someone sees through her.

We go upstairs and begin to pack. Mark brought totes and boxes, which is making everything so much easier. We mostly work in silence as if Mark can sense I need it. HE is here with us, watching everything. I can feel the sadness and despair coming from him. I choke back a sob and can't stop the tears flowing. Mark gives me a hug and asks if I need a break. I don't. I want to get this part over with. HE comes over and pushes my hair back and caresses my face when Mark has his back turned. I bite down hard on my bottom lip, trying to swallow the growing lump in my throat. A tear runs silently down my face, and I wipe it away, quickly and angrily. I shouldn't have to be saying goodbye. We deserve more time together. This isn't fair. The pain in my chest is growing, and it feels like my heart is being squeezed too tightly. I dig my nails into my hand, hoping that pain will help me hold it together. HE has his hand on my back as I survey all the packing we have done. This is it. The last of it.

"I will take these down and buy you a little time to say goodbye."

"Thank you, Mark. I will be down in a bit." I say as he closes the door behind him.

"I don't know how to say goodbye to you," I cry.

"Please…do not, Olive. Do not walk away from us," his voice cracks, raw and desperate in the recorder.

"I have no choice. They are making me move. Grandmother is making me go. I don't want to leave you. I love you, and this is killing me." He pulls me into an embrace, his masculine scent surrounding me.

"I do not know how to breathe without you. I do not even remember who I was before you loved me. I do not want to. Olive, I cannot lose you."

"I don't know what to do. I can't stay."

"You are my heart, my reason, my everything, my Olive. Please do not make this goodbye forever." He begs.

"This is not a goodbye forever. I will figure out a way to free you, and I will be back to do that. I swear to you I will. We will be together again." He pulls me into a desperate kiss right before there is a knock at the door. Time seems to stand still as I slip from his embrace and open the door. The room is heavy with words spoken and unspoken and with a love that seems to be unraveling.

Chapter 33: HIM

I follow Olive downstairs with Mark to the officer talking to the old man at the front door.

"Bye, Olive. I hate you're leaving like this," the old man says.

"Granddad, why couldn't you stick up for me…ever?" she pleads.

"Olive, I have always said I won't get into a fight or go to jail for anyone. I'm sorry."

The look on Olive's face breaks my already breaking heart further, and fury begins to build within me from his words. Mark apparently has the same reaction I do because he says, "Come on, Olive. These people do not deserve you. You have always been too good for them."

While I am glad he said that, I should be the one standing up for her. I feel worthless in this moment.

I walk with her as she goes to the moving truck with my hand on her back. I do not know when I will be able to touch her again, so I will take every moment I can. She gets into the car and looks at me as if she sees me, eyes full of unshed tears.

"Is he here?" Mark asks her.

"Yes", she says, eyes not leaving me.

"I promise I will take care of her," Mark tells me, and starts the truck. While I know he will, it does nothing to help my mood. I should be taking care of her. I should be taking her away from this place, these people.

I step back and push Olive's door closed just as the tears begin to roll down her face. I stand in the middle of the road watching my heart being taken from me. I drop to my knees as the truck drives out of sight.

Sometime later, I make my way back to our room, ignoring everything and everyone on my way. They will be dealt with later. In our room, it is so empty, yet it remains so full of memories of her. I go lie on the bed, on my usual side, and I swear I can still smell her here. I can still see her sitting cross legged reading or chatting with me about her day. I feel her in my arms as we watch those silly little movies she enjoys so much or when we would lie here together and do nothing at all. The silence is too loud. I can't take it. This room was ours. Every corner of it whispers her name to me. This is a museum of memories that I never meant to build.

I lie here on the bed staring at the ceiling for hours. I finally sit up on the edge of the bed. With my elbows on my knees and head bowed, the weight of the weekend settles upon me. I let my sadness unfurl through the house so everyone can feel it. In all of the memories, I have never cried for anything, and definitely not a human. The tears come slowly at first, silent and stubborn, sliding down my face as if my body did not want to admit she was really gone. As reality sets in, the dam breaks and I weep. This is not quiet and dignified. These are the sobs of someone who is unraveling. I do not know how to go on without her. I have never felt so empty, so hollow. All I can do for now is cry for my Olive. For our love. For the future we planned. For the pieces of myself that were lost when she left.

Chapter 34: Olive

When we get to Mark's house, Candy and Jennifer are there to help us move my things in and get my car. I am thankful Mark didn't ask about HIM on the way home, but I need to tell him soon.

"Hey, Olive! You look so much better today." Candy says as she hugs me.

"Don't worry, girl! Anything you need, we have you. Okay?" Jennifer tells me as she too pulls me in for a hug.

"Thank you all so much. I don't know what I would do without you."

"You never have to worry about that. We will always be here." Mark says, walking up beside me.

"Well, dinner is on me tonight as a thank you. Before you say no, it would mean a lot for me to do a little something for you guys."

"I think that we can handle a free meal," Jennifer says.

"Great! Let's get started."

We unload everything into the guest room Mark has cleared for me. While Mark and I return the moving truck, the girls go to pick up my car. We stop at a new fish and chips place that just opened up, called Codzilla's, and grab everyone some dinner. As we head home, Mark finally asks what I have been dreading.

"Olive, who was the man that I saw kill Steve?"

I take a deep breath. "I don't know his name. He is trapped on the land that the house sits on and has been there for hundreds of years."

"He is quite protective of you, obviously. Have you been able to communicate with him?"

"Yes...," I draw out the word as I look at him, puzzled by his nonchalant response, "But are you not freaked out?"

"I was at first, but I believe in things beyond our understanding. So, this just proves that for me."

"Not the reaction I thought I was going to get," I say with a soft chuckle, "but it makes things so much easier to explain."

"So, you have communicated, but he didn't give his name? He can't pass on?"

"Yes, we communicated all the time through a recorder and dreams, actually. He says he isn't a ghost. He says he was once powerful but has been cursed somehow."

"Does this have anything to do with the symbols we have been trying to find out about?"

"Yes." I look at him sheepishly.

"Olive, what if he is something bad? Something that will hurt you?"

"He won't."

"How are you so sure?"

"I just know him. Like I said, we have communicated every day and talked about everything." Mark can't truly understand our connection. I continue with confidence, "I know him, the real him."

"Please be careful, Olive. These things should be left alone sometimes."

"I can't leave this alone, Mark. I have to figure out how to free him. He doesn't deserve to be stuck like this."

"My sweet Olive, please promise to be careful."

"I will. I promise."

Just then, Jennifer knocks on the passenger window of Mark's car.

"Um, can we get our food? You guys can sit and talk, but we're starving." She laughs and heads to the front door of Mark's house. We laugh and follow behind her as we all go inside the house.

While the others were here and my mind was busy, my thoughts didn't drift to him, but as soon as I settle in for the night, he is the first thing on my mind. After all that I have been through, all I want is to be in his arms and feel safe. I am dreading sleep. I know he won't be there, and I am scared of who will be. I distract myself by quietly unpacking my things. There is a knock at my door, and I tell Mark to come in, already knowing it is him.

"I thought you were going to bed."

"I can't sleep. Not yet."

"Olive, I am not trying to overstep, but I think it would be a good thing if you took a couple of days off to recover."

"Oh no. I need to stay busy, keep my mind off of things."

"I could stay out with you. We could watch movies, shop, work at home, whatever you want."

"I feel like keeping things as close to normal as possible will be the best thing for me. Thank you, though, Mark. Seriously, you don't know how much this all means to me."

"I would do anything to make sure you are safe and happy, Olive." He kisses my cheek and walks back to his room beside mine.

I climb into bed, trying to ignore the ache in my heart at the fact that HE is not with me and may never be again. My tears are hot on my cheeks as my silent sobs shake my body. This is not fair. I should be with him now. I should be wrapped up with him in our bed. Instead, I have been forced away by people who are supposed to be my family. No. My family is the family I have created: Mark, Candy, Jennifer, and HIM. I close my eyes and beg for sleep to claim me. It finally does, but it is unrestful and disjointed. I toss and turn. I have flashes of the night before. I see HIM, but he doesn't see me. I wake up feeling worse than when I went to bed. I get up and look in the mirror. No amount of makeup will cover this. Maybe I should listen to Mark and take a couple of days. No. I know I need to keep a routine, but I also need to rest and deal with these emotions. I go to Mark, who is still in his sweatpants in the kitchen.

"Mark, is your movie and shopping offer still available?" I say quietly.

"Of course it is. I will call in and let Nicole in HR know what's going on."

"Thank you. I will go get ready."

We go downtown to some of our favorite boutique stores. We walk to the local coffee shop, and Mark treats me to a warm coffee before we head into my favorite store, The Pink Bow. I try on some of their new arrivals. All of them get Mark's approval, and before I get out of the dressing room, he pays for all of my favorite dresses.

"Mark, you didn't have to do that."

"Olive, I know that. I wanted to. You deserve to be treated, and I am going to do that today."

"Thank you. I really do appreciate it." I say shyly. I'm not used to someone spoiling me without ulterior motives. I know Mark's intentions are sincere, and that makes me feel cared for.

"Let's go into this store. They carry journals. I noticed yours looked well used while we were moving, and you may need new ones."

"How observant, sir." I tease, elbowing him playfully.

"I got to take care of my girl." He winks.

He wasn't lying. They carry journals, alright. They have an entire wall of them. My love of office supplies and I are going to have a field day in this store. Looking at all the new journals, I realize Mark is right, my old journal is pretty worn, so I pick out a dark emerald green one and move on to some new pens. We check out and walk around downtown, hitting the local bookstore and grocery market as well. We grab some sandwiches for lunch and head back to Mark's to watch a movie before dinner.

We choose to watch a comedy, which is a relief because I think anything else would have reminded me of HIM too much. Even this hits hard because we used to lie in bed and do this together. Before I can stop it, a tear runs down my cheek, and the movie pauses.

"Olive, are you okay?"

"Yeah, I'm fine."

"No, you're not. Please open up to me."

"I used to watch movies with HIM on the weekends, and that feeling just hit me. I promise I am okay."

"Olive, how close were you and Mr. Not Ghost?"

"Close," I say quietly.

"It's okay, Olive. I am here for you. I got you." Marks says, pulling me in for a hug.

"We can finish the movie. I promise I'm good."

When we finish the movie, we go into the kitchen and cook dinner together. Mark is such an excellent cook. I am okay, but he promises to teach me a few things. So, for now, I stick to the chopping, which I am very good at. We sit at the table and talk about our day and what we want to do tomorrow.

"I want to thank you again for everything you did for me today."

"There's no need to thank me. You deserve to be treated, Olive."

"I'm just not used to it, I guess."

“Well, get used to it, my girl,” Mark says with a big grin.

After dinner, Mark pulls out a board game to my surprise. I had told him a while ago that I had never played one, and so he bought one for us. I don’t know if he let me win, but I totally beat him. We have had the best day today, and now, I am exhausted. When I climb into bed, it doesn't take long for sleep to find me.

I dream of HIM. He is facing away from me in the garage. His midnight hair flows down his muscular back. He turns towards me slowly; his deep onyx eyes catch mine, and they are full of sadness. I reach my hand for him, and he backs away. I don’t understand. Doesn't he love me anymore? I step towards him, and he steps back again. I begin to cry and beg him to come to me, but he doesn’t. I wake up with my pillow soaked with my tears.

Chapter 35: Olive

It's been almost a month since everything happened, and Mark and I have settled into our own routine at home. We watch movies and cook together after work. He has taught me so much that I am almost as good as he is now. He has even gotten me to play video games, like we currently are now.

"You just cheated, Mark!" I yell as I throw a pillow at him.

"It isn't cheating! It's called strategy. Maybe you should learn some," he says, laughing.

"Excuse me? I was ahead of you until you shot at me!" I launch another pillow at him.

He pulls me to him and starts tickling me until we both roll off onto the floor, laughing hysterically. We sit up, and he leans over and kisses my cheek.

"I love you, Olive. You know that, right?"

"I know. You know I love you, too."

"How could you not?" He said, flashing me a smile. I roll my eyes.

"On that note, I have a video call set up with Mali in ten minutes."

"That's Kai's grandmother, right?"

"Yes. She is going to try to help me find out about those symbols."

"Olive, be careful. I know you know him now, but you don't know what he was before."

"I will be careful. I promise. I told him I would help him, and I can't stand the thought of him being stuck there." I kiss the top of Mark's head and go to my room.

I make sure I look presentable in the mirror and set up my computer for the call. I am so nervous. What if what Mark said is right? What if, after this month, HE has changed? I push all of that aside and press forward with the call.

"Hello, you must be Olive." says a beautiful older woman with sun kissed skin, dark eyes and long, grey hair braided with bits of leather.

"Hello, yes, and you must be Mali. I have heard you may be able to help me in my search with these symbols."

"Yes, I believe I can. These symbols are quite uncommon. They were only used by a group who believed they could call upon the gods and use their power to aid their people. They thought they could command the gods essentially. They sought only to help their people and were searching in any way possible to do that, even if their elders and shamans didn't agree."

“Oh wow. Why haven’t I been able to find any information on this?”

“Well, many sought to destroy it. They found it to be unnatural. I still have some information in our archives that may lead us to the answers you’re looking for. Where were these symbols found?”

“On a piece of property here in Portland. I believe that they are from the French and Indian War Era.”

“That actually makes a lot of sense to me. There have been stories passed down from those days. Many of them spoke of secret spells with special symbols, so that may be where these symbols you found are from.”

“Wow, that is all so interesting. I cannot wait to learn more. We are working on an exhibit at our museum. Do you feel it would be appropriate to include these symbols and stories surrounding them in our exhibit?”

“I would prefer that you didn’t. It was hidden for a reason, and I would like to keep them quietly shared. I will help you for your own personal curiosity, but nothing more.”

“I completely understand. I appreciate you helping me figure this out.”

“You’re welcome, dear. I will do some research in our archives, and I will get back with you before the Christmas holiday.”

"Thank you so much. I cannot wait to hear from you again."

"Goodbye for now, Olive."

"Goodbye, Mali."

This is happening. I have more information than I ever have for HIM. I'm getting so close to figuring this out, I can feel it. I wish I could tell him. I will keep this promise, though; I will free him. I go back to the living room to tell Mark what I have found out.

"So, she is still going to help you even though it's not for the museum?"

"Yes, I don't know, maybe she is happy to be researching something that not many people dig into."

"That's great, my girl. I am happy you're finally getting somewhere."

"Thank you. I think I am going to go read for a little while before bed."

"I think I may turn in myself. Come here." He pulls me in for a hug and a forehead kiss.

"Goodnight, Mark."

"Goodnight, Olive"

I go into my room and grab my work bag to get my new book I purchased out. When I do, a piece of paper falls out of the bag onto the floor. I pick it up and can't believe what it says,

"My Olive,

When the world around me falls still and quiet, and it is just me and my heartbeat, I find myself constantly thinking of you. I fear that there are not enough words to express how I feel about you, but I shall try because you deserve that and so much more.

Loving you has always felt natural, necessary. You awakened a part of me that I never knew existed within myself. I was asleep until I saw you. Every time I look into your eyes, I see home. I see our future. I see our love.

You are the calm in my fire. The light in my darkness. You are my best friend and greatest adventure. You have changed me, made me softer, stronger, fuller. Life finally makes sense with you in it. I offer you my heart, my soul, whatever you want, Olive. Name it and it is yours. Know this, my love, I will always choose you in this life and the next, and in every dream in between.

Forever yours"

Tears flow freely down my face as I try to choke back sobs. Guilt hits me hard in my stomach. I haven't even attempted to go back to him. I know I would be turned away, but I would have at least tried. I curl up in my bed, clutching the letter close, and cry myself to sleep.

Chapter 36: HIM

I do not recognize myself.

I have not left this room in ages. The days have blurred together; mornings bled into the nights, time ceasing to exist. I sit in the silence. I lie in the silence. I pace in the silence. The silence has become so loud and heavy that I cannot hear anything else, not even my own thoughts. I am not living, only existing in the space she used to be in.

I am not myself without her. I do not remember how to be anymore. She changed me. I am not the same male I was before, but now I am a hollow shell of what I was with her, and I am barely holding it together. The thing of it is, I do not want to feel better. To feel better would feel like I was letting her go, and I cannot bear to do so, even if she is already gone.

There is someone trying to get into the door again. Olive locked it and took the key with her so that I would not have to leave our room. Now the old bitch keeps trying to get in. I hear a different voice out there today. I go to inspect and find she has hired someone to break into our room. No, this will not do. Anger rises from the pit of my stomach. The first emotion other than crushing sadness that I have felt in a month since my Olive left. I leave the room, stepping close to the male as I do. I see his eyes go wide in response. I make the air around us go cold and heavy with my presence. He scampers back away and begins to mutter a prayer. I knock over his toolbox, and that does it; he runs down the stairs, screaming as he goes. That felt…invigorating. I still have the deep ache in my heart for Olive but it did feel good to scare him away. These humans have had a reprieve from my anger but that ends today. It is time to get revenge for Olive, for all the vile things they put her through, and for separating us. They will leave this place. No matter what the cost, they will leave.

A while later, the old man comes up the stairs to retrieve the man's discarded toolbox. He gathers the tools and turns back towards where I stand in the hall.

"Did you have to scare the poor man like that?"

I make the air around us frigid in response.

"I know you miss her. I cannot do anything about that."

My anger rises in response and he steps back a little.

"I will try to keep everyone out of her old room. That's the best I can do."

I step to him and he backs up.

"Just let me see what I can do okay," he turns and goes downstairs.

What does that mean? Will he try to get Olive back? Do I dare hope that could happen? No, no humans are liars and will do and say what they can to get what they want. Except my Olive, she is the only exception to that rule. She is pure and good. My light in the darkness.

After everyone retires, I make my way down to the living room and get to work making the words **BRING HER BACK** appear on the walls in the same red lettering I used before. The ogress blamed Olive then but now she cannot. I wait until 3:00 in the morning and I begin opening and slamming shut all the doors in the house. I hear a scream from their room. Perfect. The witch herself runs out into the living room and sees the writing and screams again. The old man follows her into the room and shakes his head and huffs.

"What is this? What does this mean?" she screeches.

"Well, I believe we have a spirit in the house and its angry Olive is gone."

"We have a ghost? Why haven't you said anything? Olive? Why Olive?"

"I believe we do. Would you have believed me before this? I think the spirit is uh, well, infatuated with Olive."

"Of course I would believe you! One of my closest friends is a medium. I will call her and we will deal with this. Obviously, this ghost has poor taste in women." I push over a tall lamp to the floor in front of her.

“I don’t think that’s a good idea. Whoever this is, isn’t a regular spirit. It feels more powerful.”

“Well, I am calling my friend. I want it out of my house, especially if it wants Olive here.”

With that, the hag goes back to their room and the old man lets out a sigh and follows, shutting the door quietly behind him. This is good. Let her call in this medium. I have dealt with this kind of thing before. If they are truly gifted, they will sense I am not to be trifled with.

Chapter 37: Olive

It has been almost a week since I found the letter. I read it every night, and every night, I cry myself to sleep. I need to find a way into the house. I drove by there earlier this week, hoping Grandmother would be gone and I could convince Granddad to let me visit, but she was there. I have to find a way to tell him I am close to discovering his curse.

"Hello, we're here!" Candy calls from the front door, pulling me from my thoughts.

"Come on in! Olive and I are in the kitchen," Mark answers.

"Holy shit, you guys have been busy! Look at all this! We are going to have leftovers for days!" Jennifer says, admiring the spread Mark and I put together for Friendsgiving.

"Mark has been helping me fine tune my cooking skills, so we put my learning to work on…well, all the things," I say with a chuckle.

"Aren't you two just the cutest!" Candy says as she arranges the desserts she and Jennifer brought. Mark kisses the top of my head as he walks by.

"We are, aren't we?" he says with a wink in my direction.

"Let's eat, everyone!" Jennifer says enthusiastically.

Everyone grabs their plate, and we sit around the table eating and chatting. I sit back admiring my friends. Never would I have imagined I would have found my people in my lifetime. I have always felt like an outsider, a loner. No more, though. I feel valued, loved.

"Who brought the pumpkin pie?" Mark asks.

"I did. Why?" Jennifer replies.

"That explains why it tastes like that." He says, laughing.

"Hey! That's my Nana's recipe, *Pumpkin Surprise*. Fun fact, the surprise is emotional trauma," she quips back.

"Well, it worked. I need therapy and Tums." I say laughing.

"Oh no! I had two pieces. Do I have double the issues now?" Candy says, pointing to her empty plate, giggling.

"To toxic pies and chosen family!" Mark says.

We are sitting around in the living room laughing and having a great time when my phone rings. Mark has his arm around me and looks at me questioningly.

"It's my Granddad."

"What could he possibly want after what he said to you?"

"I don't know. I'm not answering."

"You aren't curious?" Mark asks.

"Yes, but I don't want to ruin our good day."

My phone rings again and again. So, I step into my room to take it.

"Yes?"

"Olive, thank you for answering."

"Well, you called 3 times in a row."

"I really need you to come over here. Our friend is...angry."

"Oh, you think? I wonder why that is."

"I know I failed you, Olive, but I'm trying to save your friend. Your grandmother is calling in a medium to make contact and clear the house." My heart stops. No, no, no.

"Grandmother will never let me in."

"She left today to visit your aunt, and she will not be back until Sunday. You will have until Saturday to warn them and help them prepare."

"I will be there in an hour."

I hang up and pack a bag. I call Mark in and explain what is going on, and while hesitant, he understands why I have to go. I say goodbye to everyone and head over to HIM.

I walk in the door and immediately notice how heavy the air is. It feels like something is sitting on my chest, making it hard to breathe. I go into the living room where Granddad sits in his chair. He looks older, tired. Then I notice the walls. BRING HER BACK is written in red all over them.

"Maybe they will let me rest now that I have done what they wanted."

"I will stay out of your hair and will be gone Saturday." I turn and head to our room. When I go to open the door, there is some resistance, like someone pushing against it.

"It's me. Let me in, love." The door swings open, and I am pulled into his warm, masculine scent. I start to cry, and I feel him nuzzle his face into my neck. I pull away only to shut and lock the door, and then I am pulled back into him.

"I only have two days here until my grandmother comes back, and then I will have to leave again." He pulls away, grabs my hand, and leads me to the bed. We lie down, and he wraps his arms around me. I have missed this.

We wake in our dreamstate and just look at each other, almost like we cannot quite believe this is really happening. I lift my hand and touch his face, tracing his strong jaw. I look into his eyes again and see that they are already wet.

"I don't know how to change things," I say in almost a whisper.

"I know. I need to feel you again at least once more, Olive. Just once more."

Our lips meet, not urgently. This is aching, slow, reverent. We kiss like we know we are running out of time, tasting every second like it is our last. His hands roam my body like he is memorizing it, like it is sacred.

We undress in silence. The only sounds are our breaths and heartbeats. He climbed over me slowly, brushing his knuckles down my cheek. "You are the only thing that has felt like home, my Olive." He whispers in my ear. Tears slip from the corners of my eyes as he enters me, both of us gasp from pleasure and from the pain we know is coming. Our bodies move in a slow rhythm, and he holds my face the whole time, kissing my lips, my cheeks, my forehead. Whispering "I love you" like a prayer the entire time. When we fall apart together, neither of us move.

"If this is the last time…please don't ever forget me," I whisper, trying to hold back a sob.

"Never. Even if I tried, Olive. Never."

Chapter 38: HIM

We lay here in each other's arms for a long while. I have missed her more than any words could ever express. I know that this will end and she will leave again, but for now, she is here and I want to spend every second like this with her.

"I have news on the research I have been doing."

"You are still looking to free me?", I ask quietly, nervously.

"Of course I am! I am not giving up on you. On us."

"I just thought…never mind."

"That I forgot about you? Never."

"Never." I kiss her head.

"I spoke to one of the curators of the museum in Burlington and she seems confident she knows where the symbols come from."

"I trust you, Olive. I know you will be the one to free me."

"I will do my best. I promise. Have you remembered anything else?"

"I wrote down a dream I had for you before I knew you would not be returning. I dreamt I was called to a village where a grey haired male waited for me, smiling."

"Are you sure you were called?" she asked with an odd look on her face.

"Yes. I was in darkness but I believe I was somewhere I cannot remember and then there was chanting. I was pulled to the male who was chanting."

"Hmm," was all she commented.

"What do you think that means?"

"I honestly don't know."

We speak no more about my dream or research tonight. We just lie here wrapped around one another. She tells me of all the things she has been busying herself with. I must admit it stings to know that she has so much beyond me. For me, there is only her. When she is not here, I cease to be who I am with her. I am nothing but a shell, existing. She has friends. She has Mark. I am nothing. I cannot compete with the things they can do with and for her. I push all of this from my mind. Now is not the time to think of these things. Now is the time to enjoy every second I have with Olive.

She pauses speaking and I fill the pause with a kiss to her soft, full lips. The taste of her is warm and inviting. She runs her tongue lightly over my bottom lip, sending a shiver down my spine. I deepen the kiss and time seemed to stand still. The only thing that mattered is the melting sensations that is coursing through our bodies. We break the kiss, breathless, eyes reflecting our desire for each other. I flip her onto her hands and knees. I gently brush her hair over and slowly kiss down her back. My hands find her hips and my fingers dig in just enough to make her gasp.

"You have no idea how long I have wanted to do this, Olive."

"Then don't wait any longer. Take what's yours." She rubs her perfectly round bottom against me and spreads her legs.

My resolve breaks. I line up to her entrance and find she is more than ready for me. I thrust into her fully, grabbing her hips as I do. Our bodies meet with desperate need. I tangle my hand into her hair as she lets out the sweetest moans that only urge me on more. With every thrust, I whisper her name like a prayer, like a curse, like I cannot get enough. The only sounds in our dreamstate are the sounds of the rhythm of our bodies and the urgent moans of two people who need to feel everything. This could be the last time, and nothing else matters. After we come undone together, she lies beside me with her head on my chest, and we lie there until we both wake with a startle.

Chapter 39: Olive

We both jolt awake at the sound of Grandmother's yelling at the bottom of the stairs. No, no, no! She is back already! I was supposed to have two days, not one night. It's not enough time with him. I throw on my nightgown and head to the top of the staircase.

"She needed to pick up a few things I found in the garage, and it was late, so I suggested she stay in the guest room." Granddad lied. I'm shocked, honestly, but it is as much for himself as it is for me, I guess.

"Well, it's morning. Get rid of the cow," she spits.

Granddad looks up at me and nods. So, I turn around and go back to my old room. I go in and begin to change clothes.

"I have to go now that she is back. I promise I am going to fight to free you." The recorder clicks.

"I know you will, my Olive. We will be together again. I know this."

I gather my things, and he pulls me into one last hug and kiss. I turn and head down the stairs.

"You thought you could weasel your way back in, did you? Well, it won't work. You are out of this family, finally! Your little ghost friend is next. I have a friend coming to take care of that problem."

Grandmother gloats from the doorway to the living room. Suddenly, she is shoved back, and I laugh.

"Good luck with that. As far as this family, I have never been a part of that. You made sure of that yourself a long time ago. Goodbye, Grandmother." I turn and walk out the door, slamming it as I go.

There is so much more that I could say, but what good would it do? She wouldn't listen or understand it. It would be a waste of my energy and time. I have wasted enough of both on a family who doesn't want me. I have a family now who want and love me the way I deserve, and that is all I need.

I pull up to Mark's house with mixed emotions. I am sad because I had to leave HIM, but so happy we got that time together. I am feeling hopeful for the first time in a long time, if ever, that things are going to work out for me and I will get my happy ending like I have always dreamt of. Mark meets me at the door as I walk up.

"Is everything ok? I thought you were there until tomorrow?" Mark asks worriedly.

"Everything is fine. Grandmother got back earlier than Granddad thought, so I had to leave. Let's go make breakfast, and I will tell you everything."

We cook as I fill him in on everything, well, almost everything, and he is so proud of me for standing up to Grandmother.

"I'm glad you are being so positive about this. What about this friend she is bringing in? Do you think they can actually do anything?"

"No, he assured me that people have had every kind of priest and medium in the house and that none could get rid of him. He said they actually made him stronger for a while. Which won't bode well for Grandmother, honestly."

"Can you imagine her face when things get really crazy and her plans blow up in her face?" Mark jokes, and we both laugh.

"How would you feel about fighting some Black Friday crowds for a few last minute sales?" I say with a wag of my eyebrows.

"I would say, your car or mine?"

"I knew you would be in," I say with a chuckle.

Chapter 40: HIM

It has been a week since my Olive came to visit me. I thought I would sink back into the deep depression I was in before, but I have not. I am hopeful. I know she is working on freeing me and has not forgotten about me. She is safe, even if it is with Mark. I am glad she has friends who are able to be there while I cannot. Even if one of them is the male. She is taken care of, and I trust her when she says they are just friends. I am, however, still angry at the old man and old bitch that still reside here, so I will make them miserable while I wait for my Olive to return to me.

Today, they are cleaning the kitchen. I emptied the contents of every shelf in every cabinet, including the refrigerator, onto the floor last night while they were sleeping. I am currently filling this space with as much anger and aggression as I can and they are feeling it. They have been arguing since three o'clock this morning.

"It's not a good idea to have your friend over. It is already pissed Olive left."

"I don't care. I am getting rid of it tonight! I am sick of living this way."

"It is because you made Olive leave."

"She killed my best friend! It's like you don't even care!"

"They ruled it an accident."

"It wasn't. Besides, after tonight, we won't have to worry about this ghost anymore. We are going to make contact and boot it out of my house!" The stupid hag stomps off, leaving the old man to finish cleaning. I laugh to myself at her idiocy.

"I hope you have had fun keeping us up every night this week."

I have actually. I cross my arms, lean against the counter, and watch the old man sweep.

Later that evening, six of the crazy bitch's minions show up with food and candles. Are they trying to exorcise me or have a potluck with me?

I watch the women set up their food in the kitchen and eat while discussing the upcoming events for the evening. It is all your run of the mill techniques on how to rid yourself of a spirit. Ouija, seance, sage…yawn. I wish Olive was here to see this. She would quite enjoy what I was going to do this evening.

"Alright, ladies, Deb is going to show us how to set up the living room, and we will get started," the old witch bitch tells her friends.

"First, I am giving everyone crystals that I have prayed over for protection from whatever is in the house. I am sensing great evil so I would like to also say a prayer and sage everyone before we get started as well," this Deb explains. I wouldn't say I was evil but I just sit in the old man's chair and watch this show.

"I knew there was evil in this house! I just know that it was that fat little weirdo Olive that brought it here!"

I stand up and slap her face, leaving a red mark from my hand.

"Do not provoke the entity! It is obvious that it has some sort of liking to her, so I would avoid degrading her," chastises Deb.

I may like this one even if she is trying to get rid of me.

"Now, let's start with the Ouija board. Light the candles and turn out the lights."

"This is spooky," one of the minions says.

"It is important not to show fear. Some entities feed off of that. So be sure to stay calm. Now let's get started. I need one person to help me use the pointer." Deb instructed, and of course, the hag herself was the first to volunteer.

"Ok, Spirit, I know you are here, and I would like to help you if I can. Is there anything that you need help with?" Deb asks.

I move the planchette, spelling out O-L-I-V-E.

"You need help with Olive. Okay, what do you need with Olive?" Deb asks again.

B-R-I-N-G H-E-R B-A-C-K

"HELL NO! Are you kidding me? After what she did? What she accused Steve of, and then she killed him!", the old banshee screeches.

"Stay calm. Do not provoke it." Deb warns. Too late.

I take the planchette again and spell out I K-I-L-L-E-D H-I-M. All of the women's eyes go wide, and someone is screaming. I laugh. Oh, this is so much fun already, and we are just getting started.

"What can we do to move you on? You are a ghost and need to move on to your next life." Deb redirects.

N-O-T D-E-A-D. Their silence is deafening. Also, hilarious. I manage enough energy to manifest behind the old goblin, and all her friends scream. I am not fully showing myself, just a shadow, but still effective. I disappear and make the candles flare, earning more screams. The old man comes running in, and the women frantically update him on the situation.

"God dammit! I knew this was a bad idea!" he exclaims, "Everyone, stay calm. He wants Olive back. Why don't we just get her back?"

"NO! That bitch is not welcome in my house!" the troll yells.

“The pointer is moving!” Deb calls over the commotion.

M-Y H-O-U-S-E

The old man stands stunned, like he didn’t quite believe what the women had told him. He blinks a few times and then sternly says, “You ladies are finished here tonight.”

I push a breeze through the room and blow all the candles out except the ones around the board and spell out Y-O-U D-I-D N-O-T S-A-Y G-O-O-D-B-Y-E, then toss the board to the floor.

Everyone but Deb, the old man, and the old goblin queen run out the door with rushed goodbyes. I lean against a wall, arms crossed, laughing, watching the scene unfold.

“I think you need to bring in a priest. You may be looking at something demonic,” Deb says as she packs up.

“I will speak with someone when I go to church tomorrow. I have always been very religious, so this makes sense to me. The devil always targets the most righteous of the Lord’s flock,” the old ogress says smugly.

The old man and I both look at her, not believing what we are hearing. This creature is definitely not religious, and I doubt she has set foot in a church in years. I know she has not in the time she has been here.

"I suggest you do that. Until someone comes out, do *not* provoke this thing. That also means not speaking ill of Olive. It obviously has some protective feelings for her," Deb reiterates as she walks out of the front door.

"The easiest thing to do is to get Olive back here. She would not be a bother, I'm sure. You could just avoid her," the old man says as he locks the door.

"You are really that stupid. That is what this thing wants, and I will not do it. You have always had a soft spot for that girl anyway. She is just like that mother of hers, luring the men of this family into their trap and making them do whatever they want them to."

The old man sighs and walks to their room and shuts the door behind him, ending the conversation. The bitch begins cleaning up from the evening's activities, humming a tune as she does. I really hate this woman.

Chapter 41: Olive

It has been about a month since I have been with HIM. I have tried to go by, but Grandmother is always there. I have called Granddad, but he says it is too risky right now and will let me know when it is a good time to come over. Of course, there seems never to be a good time. I feel like I am going crazy. I miss him so much.

"Earth to Olive." Mark jokes, interrupting my thoughts.

"I'm sorry! I totally zoned out!" I laugh.

"I was asking what soups would you like to take to Candy's Soupmas party?" he chuckles.

"I completely forgot about that. I'm not big on holidays, so I haven't really thought about it, to be honest."

"Well, this year you are getting the princess treatment, my girl! Parties, gifts, matching pj's. The whole experience!"

"If you insist," I say, nudging him in the side.

"Since tomorrow is Christmas Eve, we'd better go grab all the things for the party and Christmas Day," Mark suggests.

We head to the crowded stores and complain about the last minute shoppers, even though we are also the last minute shoppers. We decide on making chili with cornbread for the party. So, we pick up the ingredients for that and our dinner for Christmas Day and head back home as soon as we can.

The moment we get home, my phone rings. My heart leaps thinking it is Granddad saying I can finally visit, but it is Mali. That is just as exciting, though. We have spoken a couple of times this month, but have had little progress in figuring out how to free HIM. Of course, she doesn't really know that is what I'm trying to do.

"Hi, Olive. Is this a good time?"

"Yes, it's perfect."

"I have found some information on our symbols. There is an old story I would like to tell you. I do not know the truth in it, as there is very little written about it, and the rest I put together by things passed down from my family."

"I would absolutely love to hear it."

"During the French and Indian War, a desperate elder of my tribe created a seal to summon a god to help the tribe fight to free themselves and their lands from being taken over. According to the story, a god did actually respond, but he was not what they expected, and from their hope, chaos sprang. There were great fires and great loss of lives on all sides.

While the tribe was able to stay, it was not what they expected. The elder who had summoned the god was killed in the battle, and the seal was destroyed. The god was trapped. Though no one could see him, they could feel him and his anger. The tribe tried to stay on their lands but eventually moved on because they believed the lands were now cursed. The thought was that, because the seal containing the name of the god was destroyed, he forgot who he was and how he was trapped and had become very angry. Some said he was always angry and hated all humans. I pieced what I could of the symbols together and believe I have a name of the god that was said to be summoned. Of course, the seal is not complete and never will be. However, knowing what I know, it is fairly clear who the story is about."

"Who?" I ask, trying to steady my voice.

"I don't dare say his name aloud. I am far too superstitious, but I will text it to you. I do ask that you immediately delete it. I can tell you this. He is the God of War and Chaos."

"Thank you so much for helping me get to the bottom of the symbols. What a fascinating story behind them! Obviously, I would never use this information without permission, but it does give me a more personal look at how things were during those times." She has no idea how personal this is.

"You are very welcome, dear! Please come visit when you get a break from work and this snowy weather!"

“Absolutely, I will! Mali, thank you from the bottom of my heart! I can’t wait to see you in person.”

“Goodbye, Olive.”

“Bye, Mali.”

I end the call and slowly sit on the edge of my bed. What the fuck am I supposed to do with this information? A text comes through. It's his name. HIS name. I know Mali said that she couldn’t be 100% sure, but I know this is HIM. I know it deep in my soul that this is HIS name.

Tears involuntarily run down my face. What should I do? All I have wanted is to free him, and now knowing WHO he is, I'm asking myself if it is the responsible thing to do? I promised him. I want to be with him. Could I *really* be with him, though? Would he *really* choose me? I mean, he is a literal god, and I am a chubby, nerdy human woman. I couldn’t handle freeing him and being rejected like that. Is that all he wants me for? He does hate humans. Am I just a means to an end? I can’t breathe. I’m panicking. I am trying to catch my breath and can’t. I’m getting dizzy. The room is spinning. I stand up to get Mark, and everything goes black.

I open my eyes slowly. Mark is here beside me on the phone with someone, he sounds upset.

“I heard a thump and found her on the floor. Please send an ambulance! She is unconscious. Wait! She is waking up. Thank God! Olive, are you okay? Don't worry. Help is coming."

"I'm ok. My head hurts a little." I rasp.

"It's ok, sweet girl, I think you hit it when you fell. The paramedics are at the door and I will be right back."

"No, I'm ok." I try to sit up and immediately regret it. It's too late though. He has already left the room.

The next thing I know the paramedics rush in and begin checking my vitals and checking me over.

"Miss, I recommend that you go to the hospital to be monitored since you passed out and could have hit your head," one of the paramedics explains.

"Okay," I say tentatively, looking at Mark who is standing back watching with a worried look.

"I will ride with you. I will call Jennifer and ask her to pick us up when they release you," he reassures me.

We ride to the hospital, and once we are there, we get settled into the emergency room. The doctor comes in to check me over and ask questions about what happened before I passed out.

"What happened before you passed out?" she asks.

"I had been sitting on the bed, and I started feeling like I was having a panic attack. It was hard to breathe, and I started to feel dizzy. I stood up to get Mark and that is all I remember."

"I heard her fall and rushed in to check on her. I found her lying close to the bedside table and was afraid she had hit her head," Mark adds.

"I would like to admit you for a CT scan, some bloodwork, and I would like to monitor your heart just as a precaution," the doctor explains and leaves the room.

"I am so sorry, Mark! I hope we don't miss Candy's party because of me."

"Hey, don't apologize. You can't help this, Olive. I have already texted her and Jenn and let them know what is going on and that we may be late to or miss Soupmas."

"Soupmas", I laugh, "Candy and her party ideas."

"Oh, come on, Olive. She is soup-er excited about this one," we both laugh and Mark takes my hand, his expression turning serious, "I know who you were talking to and what it was about. I won't force you, but you can tell me anything, Olive."

"I know, Mark. I need to understand it myself before I can ever explain it. It's…a lot."

"Just know I am here, babe," he says, kissing my hand.

I finally got through all the tests and labs and into my room for the night. I am exhausted, mentally, physically, and most of all emotionally. I am so confused about what to do. Not that I can do anything right now anyway, because I can't even get to the property without Grandmother knowing. All I can do now is prepare myself to free him and then decide what to do later. What I need to do at this moment is sleep and feel better so I don't let my friend down tomorrow. I scoot over in the bed to make a space for Mark.

"Come on. The bed is more comfortable than that recliner."

"You don't have to beg me, Olive. Of course, I will sleep with you," Mark smirks and winks.

He climbs into bed, and I curl up to him. We talk for a few minutes and then we both are drifting off to sleep. In the morning, the doctor comes in and says that my heart tests and overnight heart rates were great, and she felt comfortable releasing me as long as I took it easy over the next couple of days. Mark assured her he would make sure I did just that.

"Hey, Jenny," Mark holds the phone from his ear, and I can hear Jennifer fussing at him for calling her that from where I am sitting, "Sorry, sorry. Listen, we are going to be able to go in a bit. Could you come get us and take us home...I know it's just for Olive…Thanks." He gets off the phone laughing.

"You'd better watch it. She kept threatening people with that gin bottle at Halloween. It was very specific, so I think she has used that move before."

"Noted," he chuckled.

Jennifer drops us off at home so we can get ready for the party this evening. Mark gets the chili going in the slow cooker while I shower and do my hair and makeup. While he showers, I get the cornbread started. I just can't sit there and let him do all the work.

"Olive. Seriously, you're supposed to be sitting and taking it easy." Mark comes out with a towel wrapped low on his hips and his hair a wet mess of waves. I try not to look, but I fail, and he clocks it. His mouth upturns in a slow grin, "Like what ya see, babe?"

"Oh, shut up! I can't just sit here and let you do all the work. I need to be distracted too."

"One, I can distract you. Two, I am here if you need to talk. You know I know about HIM."

"I may take you up on the distraction later, but for now, I think you're right, and I need to talk this out."

He goes and slides on some pants and sits at the bar while I work on the cornbread recipe. I give him the short version of events, leaving out HIS name. When I am finished, Mark just looks at me and takes a deep breath.

"He is a literal god. Like, seriously?"

"Apparently. I don't know what to do. I promised him I would help, but what if I unleash something horrible on the world?"

"I understand. I think you would be wise to wait for a bit. I mean, he has been here for over 250 years. A bit longer won't hurt him."

"You're right. I need just to think this through."

"Of course, I'm right. Come here, Doll. You're not alone in this. I'm here for you." He pulls me in for a hug and kisses the top of my head.

We get to Candy's house, and everything feels so warm. She has decorated simply with a tree by the window, warm white twinkle lights strung around the living room, and a small fire in the fireplace. The smell of all the simmering soups and quiet conversations just warm the party even more. Mark puts our food in the kitchen while I talk to Candy and Jennifer.

"I'm so glad your tests came back ok and you were able to be here tonight!" Candy exclaimed.

"Me too! I was so worried I would have to miss this."

"Olive, not trying to stress you out, but if Mark calls me Jenny one more time…"

"There's my girls and Jenny." Mark laughs, blocking the slap on the arm Jenn sends his way.

"Mark, it's Soupmas. Give her a break for the night." I joke.

"Okay. In honor of Soupmas." He says with a laugh.

"Who made the spicy chili? I think my sinuses have been cleared for the next year!" Candy quips.

"You're welcome. It's called 'Cleansing by Fire.'" Marks says. We all laugh.

"I brought the French Onion, but I forgot the onion…it's just French," Jennifer comments.

"So, you brought wine," I say dryly. Everyone erupts in laughter.

The rest of the evening is full of laughter, friendship, and everyone cozied up by the fire. It's actually perfect. I don't believe I have ever said that about my life before. I feel like everything is falling into place. Except HIM. I miss him. I wish he were with me. As if he can read my thoughts, Mark puts his arm around me and asks if I need that distraction. I give him a playful shove and laugh.

We head home later that night, and Mark says he has a surprise for me. When we get in the house, he hands me a gift. I open it and it is a set of pajamas and my favorite Christmas movie, Elf.

“I got us matching pajamas and thought we could watch a movie and have snacks before bed.” He says quietly, almost like he is afraid I will reject his idea.

“This is perfect, Mark! No one has ever done anything like this for me. Thank you so much.”

“You deserve this and so much more, Olive. You are kind, accepting, smart, and you have a beautiful soul. Of course, you are gorgeous, but you are so much more than that. I love you, my girl.”

“I love you too.” I smile at him and pull him into a hug. I allow myself to get lost in his warmth for a second and then pull away, “Let’s get changed and start our movie!”

We pop some popcorn and set out cookies and milk for Santa. I know it’s childish, but I have never gotten to do things like this before now. So, to me, it’s fun. We get a big blanket and cuddle up on the sofa and turn the movie on. We get halfway through, and I am asleep.

I wake up snuggled up next to Mark and at the table in front of me, covered in gifts. I sit up and look around. While I was sleeping, he laid out our gifts on the coffee table, ate the cookie, drank the milk, and even left a cheesy note from Santa. I start to tear up and look at him. He is looking at me already.

“Oh no, don’t cry, my sweet girl.” He pulls me back into him and holds me for a moment.

"I have never felt so loved and cared for. I am just so happy."

"Good. That's what I want you to feel every day. Now let's open our gifts!" He says with a big smile.

Of course, he got me thoughtful gifts. There was this journal set I saw online. He remembered and ordered it. I saw a vintage bracelet at a jewelry store in town that matched the necklace he got me, and he bought it. I can't believe this man. If I didn't know better, I would think he was actually in love with me. He is just so thoughtful. It would be so much easier if he were. No curses, no games, no stress; but then I wouldn't have HIM, and I can't imagine that.

After we open our gifts, we cook a huge breakfast and spend the rest of the day lying around watching movies, just laughing and napping. It has been the best day. I can't help but to feel guilty for being so happy.

Chapter 42: HIM

It has been another long month without my sweet Olive. I need her back. It is like there is no air without her here. I have enjoyed tormenting these humans and creating chaos when I can, but it doesn't fill the void that is left when she is gone.

The humans celebrated Christmas a few days ago. Of course, I did not let them do so peacefully, but they celebrated nonetheless. The old banshee sang songs and hymns by the piano, which was such torture to everyone present that I did not have to do much to make them miserable. She has become quite involved in the church since her little gathering. Today her priest will be here to try to clear the house of me. They will try, just as others have before, but they will fail, just as the others did. I am no mere spirit they can cleanse this house of. I have seen those come and go in my time here. I am much stronger.

The priest is shown into the living room, and they all sit and begin to speak about my activities. Well, I suppose it is showtime. I make the lights flicker. The priest asks about the wiring, and the old man informs him that the wiring is not the issue. Okay, this male needs something bigger. The air in the room grows cold. So cold, I see the priest shiver. He stands and begins to pray and sprinkle holy water around the house. I follow him to make sure he is doing it properly.

"Spirit, I command you to leave this darkness and go toward the light. Leave this house." Bold of him to presume that he can command me to do anything. The only light I will go to is Olive. I need to make that very clear. So, I make her name appear on the mirror in front of him. His eyes go round and fear rolls off of him.

"Who is Olive?"

"It is our granddaughter. Sweet girl, but I believe she dabbled in the occult before I had to make her leave this house." Lying to a priest. When I did not believe this she devil could surprise me anymore, she does this.

"I see…Olive is no longer here. You need to go back from which you came." The priest says, sprinkling more holy water. I walk over to the wall where the old hag has hung several crosses and start spinning them. That usually gets these guys really upset. The priest looks as though he may vomit. Apparently, the church has sent a greenhorn to try to deal with me. I am rather insulted.

"Th..the power of…", he tries to get out another command as I begin to flicker the lights again. He flicks holy water toward the nearest light, and there is a loud pop as the water hits the outlet. I start laughing so hard that they are actually able to hear me. I am as shocked as they are. The priest tries and fails at gathering his composure. They all go to the foyer.

“So, you are just going to leave this unfinished?!”, the banshee screeches.

“This is beyond what you initially described, Mrs. Ambrose. I need to consult with the church and get assistance. I will be here for you every step of the way. I just cannot do this alone.”

“Of course I understand. Thank you for coming out. I will continue my prayers, you showed me.”

“I will contact the church immediately and will be in touch as soon as I hear back. Call me if anything new happens.” With that, the priest leaves.

“I can’t believe him. All the work I have been doing for the church, and he can’t even help us.” She says, throwing her hands in the air.

“I don’t think that’s how this works. He probably hasn’t seen many cases like ours in this area, is all,” the old man says.

“Oh, so you're defending him and his incompetence?”

“Just forget it. I’m going to watch some television.”

She storms off to their room, and the old man sits in his chair. I turn the TV on to the channel he was watching earlier.

“Thanks”

I sit too, because what else do I have to do? I wonder what Olive is doing now. Is she reading one of her naughty little books? Are her cheeks flushed with color because she is turned on? Is she thinking of me? Is she with Mark? I stand up and begin to pace. She said they are just friends, and I believe her. I do. My mind drifts to the what ifs, though. What if she seeks comfort in his arms? What if he convinces her that there is no future with me, and she gives up and settles for him?

"If you are going to be angry, can you do it somewhere away from me, please?" the old man asks me.

Why does everyone think they can command me today? No. I will stay right here and be angry. It is partly his fault that Olive is not here. I turn the television off.

"I take that as a no," he says and gets up, heading to the garage. I follow. I am tired of everyone thinking that they can speak to me as if this were their house. This is my house. My land. Olive is mine, and they made her leave. I am done.

I rush in front of him, blocking the door. I am so full of rage at everything and everyone. Right now, the old man is the one here. I close my eyes, lower my head, and take a deep breath, trying to channel all of my anger. I look up and he is staring at me. He can see me. For a second, we look at each other, and then I speak.

"Bring her back. Bring my Olive back to me."

"I…I…I.." The old man stutters and then grabs his chest. He falls, sending some pots that were on the countertop to the floor.

"NO! You have to bring her back." I roar at him.

"WHAT IN THE HELL!", the bitch yells as she comes stomping in. She realizes he is on the floor and rushes to his side. She looks up and sees me. She stands up and backs away from me. "You! You killed him!"

"He is not dead…yet. Call for help, you imbecile…and BRING OLIVE BACK!" I look down at the old man, who is gasping and making a gurgling noise, "All I wanted was for her to be here with me." He looks up at me in acknowledgement and draws his last breath.

"Send an ambulance! He's lying on the floor. I think he is dead! There is this ghost in the kitchen that scared him! I am looking at him right now! No, I haven't taken anything!!" the old crazy hag screams frantically into the phone. I look her in the eyes, smile, and then I will myself to disappear.

All of the emergency services the city has to offer come to the house. The paramedics confirm that the old man has passed away. The police are speaking with the witch at the moment.

“On the phone, you said there was an intruder in the house?” the officer asks.

“No, it was this ghost! He has been haunting us, and now he has killed. Why aren’t you listening to me?” she cries.

“Ma’am, I believe you might be in shock. Let's get you to the hospital to get checked out. I know this has been a traumatic evening,” the officer replies.

“Oh yes, you’re right! I do think I need to go to the hospital!” she bawls. “Can I go get my coat and boots from my room?” she then says calmly, snapping out of her melodramatics.

“Absolutely,” the officer replies kindly.

She goes to her room all right, but comes back out with what looks like a Molotov cocktail and throws it on to the living room curtains. “No one believes me! Olive and her demon pet will not have my house!” she yells as she sets the curtains ablaze.

The room explodes with action. The police officer subdues the old hag as she laughs crazily. The paramedics rush out with the old man's body, and the firefighters are quickly on top of getting the flames out. A while later, another officer comes back in with news about the bitch.

“I got in touch with the daughter and she is on her way to the hospital. It looks like they are putting a hold on the mother, and then she is going to go live with her kids. This house is in foreclosure according to the daughter, so the bank will be selling it soon anyway." I overhear the officers on scene speaking. I feel ill. Someone else will buy the house. My Olive is gone forever. I was trying to get her back and now I have lost her forever. Everything starts spinning. I do not know what to do. I sit in the old man's chair with my head in my hands.

After all of the people have gone and locked the house up, I allow myself to lose control. I smash the lamps, the figurines, whatever I can get my hands on. I fall to my knees and roar out with the pain that is in my heart, shattering the glass in the front windows. The cold from outside slaps my face with fury. I will never be with her. I will never see those beautiful, icy blue eyes, run my hands through that soft, thick, snowy white hair. Never again will I feel the warmth of her curves against my body. Hear her angelic laugh. What have I done?

Chapter 43: Olive

Mark and I are working on cataloging some new artifacts we got over the Christmas holiday, and my phone rings.

"It's my aunt. She never calls," I tell Mark.

"Do you want me to step out?"

"No, I will tell you everything anyway," I laugh, "Hello?"

"Hi, Olive. I wanted to let you know a few things that happened over the weekend. Granddad passed away from a heart attack."

"What? Oh my god. I'm so sorry. He didn't suffer, did he?"

"Other than a life with your grandmother, no, he didn't. It was very quick. Grandmother went nuts and tried to burn the house down. The firefighters were there and got it put out quickly, but apparently the windows burst from the heat or something. We went and boarded them up, though. Grandmother is going to live with your uncle in Virginia. So, we got all of her things out of the house."

"Okay…" I say wondering why that concerns me.

"I know you love that old house. I wanted to let you know that it is in foreclosure. Dad wanted you to have it, but the bank doesn't care about that. I know you have been saving, and I have asked a friend of mine to give you the first shot at purchasing it."

"Yes! Yes, I want it! Oh my god, thank you! I will go there right now!"

"Good. I am glad this worked out for you. I just wish that Dad were still here. He really did love you. He just never knew how to show any of us love well. I am sorry for none of us ever sticking up for you."

"Th…thank you."

"We aren't having any services because he didn't want a big to-do when he died. He is being cremated, and I will be keeping his ashes until we decide where to spread them."

"Thank you. I really appreciate you calling me and letting me know everything that has happened. Thank you so much for speaking with the bank."

"Goodbye, Olive."

Just like that, my biological family was out of my life. I am feeling a flurry of feelings right now, but most of all, an urgency to get to the bank.

"Mark, I have to go to the bank right now. The house is in foreclosure, and Granddad is dead. Grandmother is going to Virginia."

"Okay, breathe, babe. Let's take lunch and head to the bank. You can fill me in on the way."

We get to the bank and park. Before we can get out of the car, Mark turns to me, grabs my hand, and says, "Olive, please think about this. You don't have to do this. You could just stay with me. Instead of this being a way to him, it could also be a way out. You have been so happy. I want you to be happy."

"I have to do this. I have been dreaming of this for a while now. It is like all I have wanted is coming true. I mean, minus Granddad dying. I will have my own place. HE is there. I can finally figure out what to do about that situation and his intentions. I don't have to worry about my family ruining anything for me anymore. It will be something that is just mine."

"I'm just worried, Olive. I love you."

"I love you too. You have to admit having me with you has cramped your dating life."

"Olive, you have cramped nothing. I love having you with me. I…", he sighs, "I just want you to be safe and happy."

"I will be."

We go inside and I ask for my aunt's friend, Betty. We are led to her office, where she greets us and has us sit down.

"Your aunt was very passionate that you got the first opportunity to purchase this house. I had many resources for first buyers ready for you when you came in, but before you got here, someone came in and purchased the house." My heart sinks.

"What do you mean? I came as soon as I was told. I was supposed to have the first chance."

"Oh, you have the house, Miss Ambrose. Mr. Oliver Ambrose came in, purchased it, and put your name on the deed. The house is yours. I will have all the paperwork and keys ready after the new year."

"My father came here?" My head is spinning at all of this information.

"Yes. He said it was from a fund he and your mother, Olivia, had set up before you were born."

"Do you happen to have any contact information? I would like to say thank you."

"No, I'm sorry he did not leave any. He said everything was yours now."

"Oh, okay. Thank you."

"Here is some paperwork I need you to sign. Once it is signed, I will get everything moving, and we will have you in the house shortly after the new year. I know there was some damage from a fire in the front of the house, but Mr. Ambrose has taken care of that as well. So, it will be turnkey ready for you!"

I work on signing all the papers and hand them back over to her.

“Today didn’t go how I thought it was going to go, but thank you so much for all of your help!”

“You’re welcome, sweetie. I will call you when everything is ready for you.”

With that, Mark and I left and are headed back to work. Mark is quiet the rest of the day, but so am I. So much has happened in the past few hours. I’m not sure how to really process it. I know Mark is upset I am leaving, but I need this for myself. I can’t just stay with him forever. I want a chance at real love, happiness, a family, and a future. Staying with Mark won’t give me that. He doesn’t love me like that, nor I him. That does make me a little sad because we actually would be a good couple. I have never let myself feel that way with him because I know he would never feel that way back. It would ruin what we have, and I am not willing to risk that.

“I’m sorry I have been quiet today. I am just sad you’re going to be leaving.”

“I know. I’m sad too. I need this, though. Something for me. Even though my father bought it, it is still mine to do with whatever I want. I have never had anything like that.”

“I know. I am happy for you. I really am. I just needed to wallow in self pity for a bit.”

“I will still be with you until all the paperwork is final. Plus, we still have a New Year’s Eve party to throw. Come on, let's go have dinner. On me.”

"Don't say things like that and get my hopes up, Olive. Dinner ON you sounds so good." He winks at me.

"Shut up, you perv." I smack his arm and laugh, "Come on. Let's go."

Chapter 44: HIM

I am broken. I am not even trying to put myself back together. I have just been sitting on the floor against the wall quietly in the ruins of my life. If you can call it a life now. There is nothing for me anymore. Not without her. Not without my Olive. Someone came and boarded up the windows. I barely noticed. It is cold in this house either way. They came for that bitch's things. I let them. My fate is sealed now. No Olive. No chance at freedom to be with her. Nothing.

The front door opens, and a couple of workers come in with supplies to paint and fix the windows. I sit there and stare at the wall. What is the point of messing with them?

"The new owner is moving in by next week, so we need to hurry. They are paying us a pretty penny to fix this place up and do it right, so let's get going."

Great. The house has already been sold. New humans. New humans where my Olive should be. I cannot do this. I go back to my old space in the garage. Back to the darkness from which I came.

Sometime later, it's like I am being tortured. I swear I can feel Olive's presence in the house, hear her voice. I roll over in my space and tune everything out. I cannot take this.

Chapter 45: Olive

It's New Year's Eve and I am going out to grab some last minute things for our party tonight. I find myself in front of my new house. I don't have the final paperwork yet, but maybe the contractor working on it will let me in. I pull in the driveway and walk to the door, which is open.

"Hello, Miss, can I help you?"

"Hi, I am Olive Ambrose. I own this house. I was wondering if I could come and see the progress? If now is a bad time, I completely understand."

"No, ma'am. Come right on in and take a look around. If you see anything that needs attention, you let me know."

"Thank you so much."

I walk through the house trying to find HIM. All I feel is heartbreaking sadness. I know it is HIM, but he will not come out. Is he hiding from me? Does he not want to see me? I can't walk through and call out to him, so I pretend I am on the phone so he will hear my voice, but it doesn't work. Have I just gotten this house to be with him, for him not to want me anymore? I go to the garage and try to open the storage room door, but it is locked. I don't have keys yet, so I can't open it. I try to whisper to him, but he will not come to me. I finally give up and go back to the foreman.

"Everything looks great! Thank you so much for working so hard to get this finished quickly."

"No problem, Miss Ambrose. We are happy to do this for you."

"Well. I won't bother you anymore. Thank you for letting me take a look."

I get back to Mark's, and he has everything set up, minus the few items that I took so long to get. I apologize for taking so long; of course, he understands. I rush to get into my new dress. I chose a body hugging deep emerald green sequined short dress that highlights my curves perfectly. I'm wearing my hair in loose curls. I can't wait for Candy to see this dress since she helped me pick it out.

I walk out, and Mark stops what he is doing and stares at me for what seems like forever, "That bad?" I ask.

"No, that good. Olive, you look ravishing." I roll my eyes.

"Come here." He pulls me in front of the mirror and with his hands on my waist. "Look at yourself, Olive. You are beautiful. You are the most beautiful woman I have ever seen." For some reason, his words and the look in his eyes has warmth pooling in my stomach. Nope. Nope. Get it together, Olive. He is just being nice.

“Thank you, Mark,” I say, but it comes out almost as a whisper.

A knock at the door interrupts the moment, and I swear there is a look of disappointment on his face. Of course, Candy and Jennifer are the first ones to come through the door. I love how we all show up for each other.

“See! I told you that dress was the one!” Candy exclaimed as she walked into the room.

“You were right, as always.” That earned me a hug and a massive smile from her.

“I could use a drink. Anyone else?” Mark says.

“Sure. I would love some wine,” I answer as he goes to the kitchen to get it.

More guests arrive, and soon the party is in full swing with music, dancing, and plenty of drinking. Naturally, we have lots of mocktails and nonalcoholic options for our nondrinkers and designated drivers, too. By the end of the evening, Mark and I both had several drinks. But it's our house, so I guess that's okay. Mark and I are dancing together as the countdown to midnight starts. Before I know, it's midnight and his lips crash into mine. One of his hands slides onto the back of my neck, and the other onto the small of my back. This kiss is hungry. Deep, claiming. No one around us seems to notice. They are all cheering or watching fireworks outside.

"Happy New Year, Olive. Come on, let's go outside before they notice we are missing." Mark whispers into my mouth.

After the fireworks, people started leaving. Jennifer and Candy asked to crash on the couches. Needless to say, we said yes. Again, I saw a flash of disappointment on Mark's face. I am secretly glad they are staying, though. That kiss was confusing, and I know, in the state Mark and I are in, we would not stop at another kiss. We give a lingering look to each other and then say our goodnights and head to our separate rooms for the night.

When we wake up, Candy and Jennifer help us clean up, and we all eat brunch together. I am eternally grateful because it saves Mark and me from an awkward morning. By the afternoon, everything seems back to normal. Okay, great. It was a kiss, nothing else. No feelings. I can handle that. I think.

"About that kiss," Mark says while we are watching television.

"I wondered when we would talk about that."

"It doesn't have to mean anything if we don't want it to," he says.

"I don't know what to feel about it, especially given things you have told me in the past."

"I know I am confused about everything too," he confesses.

"Let's call it just a midnight kiss until we become less confused."

"That sounds reasonable," he chuckles.

"Then it is settled and unawkward."

"Settled and unawkward," he laughs.

The phone wakes me up after a night of restless sleep. I reach over and read the caller ID through sleepy eyes and see it is Betty from the bank.

"Hi, Olive?"

"Yes, this is her."

"Sorry to call so early, but I have your final paperwork and keys. I thought you would want them as soon as I got them."

"Yes, thank you! This is wonderful. I will be down as soon as I can."

I hang up and throw on the nearest sweater and jeans I find. I run to the bathroom and quickly do my hair and makeup.

"Hey, where are you off to so early?"

"Betty from the bank called and she has my paperwork and keys ready to go!"

"This quickly? I thought we had more time."

"I know. I'm sorry."

"It's okay. I know this is exciting for you. I'm happy for you, Olive." I can tell he halfheartedly means that, but he is trying, so that means a lot. I kiss his cheek and head out the door.

I get to the bank and meet with Betty. I try not to seem impatient while we go over the paperwork and legal wording, but it isn't easy. All I want is to get to my house and let him know I am the new owner, and I never have to leave. Although I still haven't decided to free him, I do have an idea of how to now. Poor Betty seems like she never gets to speak to anyone and keeps me there for an hour and a half. I am practically running to my car as soon as I leave her office. In my haste to leave this morning, I didn't grab clothes, blankets, food, or anything but my purse and phone. I make a quick stop by the nearest box store and grab some new sheets and blankets, some groceries, and a couple of changes of sweats.

I pull up at my house, MY house, and sit in the car for a moment and let it sink in that this is really happening. Nothing else seems to matter right now but HIM. Not my family. Not the kiss. Nothing but HIM. Us.

I walk into the house and am hit with that gut wrenching sadness. I sit everything down in the foyer and close and lock the door. I call out for him as I walk through the house. I make my way to the storage room, where I know he was last time. I open the door and am hit with a new wave of heartbreak.

"I'm here. Come out." I hear shuffling in the corner of the room, and then I am aware he is standing out of reach. "*Please*. I came as soon as I could. I couldn't stay away from you any longer. I love you." I pause and swallow the sob that is threatening to escape, "Please, still love me."

Chapter 46: HIM

I hear her again. My mind is playing tricks on me. Again. I am in my own personal Hell. Trapped in this house, in my head. I hear her louder, closer. The door opens. This is new. She is begging me to come out. I stand and turn, facing the door. I cannot believe my eyes. My beautiful Olive is standing before me like a dream I have replayed many times. Except this time, it is a reality. Begging me to come out, to love her still, as if I could ever stop. How I have missed her with my entire self, deep within whatever soul I have. Then suddenly, she is here.

She places the recorder on the shelf against the wall between us. My chest tightens, and my voice catches in my throat.

"You…you came back."

"Of course, I came back. I love you." Her eyes are full of unshed tears.

I do not care if I catch her off guard. I quickly close the space between us and pull her to me with one hand, and I manipulate the recorder with the other.

"I have been losing my mind without you, my Olive," my voice low and trembling, "I swore I could feel you here. Hear your voice."

"I came to see you, but you wouldn't come out. You locked yourself in, and I couldn't get to you. I thought…I thought you didn't want to see me."

"I thought I was hallucinating. I missed you in ways I did not know were possible, Olive. I missed your voice, your laugh, your fire. The way you make me feel like your male."

I kiss her then. I kiss her as if making up for every second we were apart. I let my hand roam her body, reclaiming what is mine and she lets me.

"Olive, please never leave me. I will never survive losing you again."

"Never," she answers.

We do not make it to the bedroom until I am on her. I cannot help it. I have longed for her. Longed for everything about her, every part of her, and right now I want to reclaim every bit of her. I pin her against a wall in the living room. My body has waited far too long to be near hers. My hands are tangled in her hair, and my mouth is tasting every bit of hers she will give. This is not just lust. This is need. This is for every lonely night and every whispered "I miss you" that she would never hear.

"I thought you hated me last time I was here." She gasped when I moved to kiss her neck. I could never hate her, and I intend to show her that.

I take her hand and lead her upstairs. She unlocks our room, and I am on her again. She pulls off her sweater, and I take off my tunic. Once our skin makes contact, it is like a storm breaking. We shed all of our clothes as we made our way to the bed. I lay her down slowly, my mouth on hers the entire time. I start kissing her neck before I kiss lower until I reach the apex between her thighs. She spreads her legs wide, naughty, greedy little thing. I give her what she wants. I have missed the taste of her. She arches into me, her breath catches, and I know she is close to release. I suck on her clit and add two fingers inside of her. She comes hard, and I am met with fresh wetness. Her moans are like music to my ears. I have missed those sounds. When I am sure she is thoroughly pleased, I line up to her entrance and thrust into her, reclaiming what is mine once again. She wraps her legs around me, urging me to go as deep as I can. I am more than happy to oblige. My movements become more and more frantic as my own release draws near. Just as I fall apart, she comes with me. She is perfect. She is mine.

I pull her into me and hold her until she dozes off. I go downstairs and hurriedly put away the cold foods I saw in the foyer and grab her a blanket. I return to our room and cover her before climbing into bed, wrapping my arm around her and falling asleep myself.

Chapter 47: Olive

We have never done that before. I'm sure it would look ridiculous if anyone saw. Since no one can see him, I don't care. I missed him so much more than I let myself feel. I love him. I am finally back in his arms, where I belong.

I wake up in our dreamstate and look up at his gorgeous face, his raven black hair splayed out on the pillow.

"Hi."

"Hello, my Olive."

"I wasn't sure if you would still want me after you wouldn't come to me that day."

"I could never stop wanting you. I will always want you, Olive. You are everything to me."

"I missed you so much."

"I miss you in ways I did not know possible, Olive. How long do we have together?"

"Forever. I own the house now." He sits straight up in the bed.

"Do not joke about this, Olive."

"I'm not joking. I own the house. It's just me and you now." He grabs my face and kisses me deeply.

When he pulls away, he has a smile on his face that makes me melt instantly. I am in trouble because I know that there is no way that I can go back on my word to free him. Still, I don't tell him anything of what I found out.

"Happiness does not begin to describe what I am feeling in this moment. I have wanted nothing more than to have you all to myself since I first laid my eyes upon you, Olive." He lies back down and pulls me close to him. I lie my head on his chest and listen to the steady beat of his heart. I draw slow circles on his skin while he brushes his hand lazily along my spine.

"Your heart is loud tonight," I say softly.

"With good reason," he chuckles. I smile against his chest, my fingers still tracing small circles.

"What do you think our future will look like?"

"Us, together until death parts us when we are old and grey. Even then, we will be reunited in what lies beyond this world."

"We have to free you first for that to happen."

"Yes, I suppose we do. Even if we never find a way, I am with you, Olive. I will always find a way to be with you. I cannot be without you again."

"What if you are free and decide you don't want me?"

"It will not happen."

"What if you realize I am not good enough because I am human?"

"It will not happen."

"What if someone comes along that is more attractive and you would rather have them?" He leans up on his elbow and looks down at me.

"This will never happen. Olive, why do you worry so? Have I given you reason to doubt my love? Please tell me if I have, because I assure you, I will correct it. I love you, my Olive. I have loved you since the moment I laid eyes on you, and no one will ever come close to the way that you make me feel. You are my forever, Olive."

I am silent for a second, tears catching in my lashes. He leans in, resting his forehead on mine. Then he kisses me. Not to spark something or to tease, just to say he is mine. When he pulls away, I smile, truly smile.

"You have never given me a reason to doubt you. I just worry that once you regain your memories, you will realize that you are better off without me around. I love you so deeply. I would not be able to take you rejecting me."

"You never have to worry about that, my Olive. I would rather cease to exist than to not have you as mine." He leans down and gently kisses me. I go to turn toward him and rub against him with my thigh.

"Oops," I say innocently.

"You are testing my self control, Olive." I lean in and brush my lips against his jaw.

"I don't know what you mean." I teasingly whisper.

"If you are trying to drive me crazy, my Olive, you are succeeding."

"Then why aren't you doing anything about it?" In one motion, he rolls us over, pinning me beneath him. He kisses me deep, hungry, like he has been holding back. My hands slide into his silky hair and pull him closer. He lets out a low moan at my roughness.

"You are not getting out of this bed until we forget what day it is." He says in a low tone.

"Then maybe I should tease you longer," I say breathless and smiling. I do continue to tease him, too. Every touch and kiss don't quite lead where he wants it to, and finally, his patience snaps. When it does, there is nothing playful about the way he claims me.

His mouth trails down my throat, slow and unhurried, tasting my pulse with a kind of worship. My breath catches, fingers gripping his back, nails digging in just enough to make him groan low against my skin. He bites down slightly on my neck, eliciting a moan from me.

"Please, don't hold back." He lifts his head just enough to meet my eyes.

“I was not planning to,” his voice rough with heat.

The kiss that follows his confession is ravenous. His hands slide down, gripping my thighs, parting them slowly. I shift beneath him, panting as my body arches to his touch, my hips lifting in silent invitation. He is taking his time. It is slow, torturous. His fingers glide over my clit, slow and circular motions, learning my every reaction, my every sigh. My body trembles as he maps me with patience and precision. When he finally slips inside of me, the stretch is slow and deliberate. I gasp, and it is swallowed by his kiss. He rests his forehead against mine, our breath tangled. There is nothing frantic in our movements. They are deep and rhythmic. I wrap my legs around him and urge him deeper. He groans low and raw.

“Olive,” he moans like a prayer, lips brushing against my ear.

My nails drag along his spine. My body rocking with his, every thrust pulling moans from both of us that mix perfectly with the creak of the bed. The heat builds, coiling tighter, our hearts pounding in unison. As our climax hit us, he kisses me through it, his hand sliding under my thigh pulling me as close, as deep as he can. Our bodies are slick and locked in rhythm with each other as the pressure threatens to break us apart. He buries his face in my neck and we stay just like this for a long moment, bodies tangled, skin damp, breath steadying against each other.

No words are needed right now. He finally pulls back, and I see his messy hair, swollen lips, eyes soft and shining. He is smiling. God, I love his smile. God, I love him.

Chapter 48: HIM

We wake up from our dreamstate and lie in each other's arms in the morning light for a while. I hear her soft snores, and I know she has drifted back to sleep. I carefully get up and go downstairs. I know that she loves a cup of coffee in the morning, and now that it is just her and me in the house, I am able to move things freely. I make her coffee and soon hear her light footsteps coming toward the kitchen.

"You made me coffee?"

"I remember you like to have it in the mornings." I am glad I got the recorder out this morning.

"You memorized how I like my coffee?"

"Of course. Why would I not? I try to remember everything I can about you, Olive."

"You are the best. Mmm, this is wonderful. Thank you, love."

"What do we need to do today? I would like to help get you settled."

"I need to go set some things from Mark's. I need to order some furniture, groceries, curtains, blinds, all the things." She laughs. I tense at Mark's name but take a deep breath and shake it off.

"I will do whatever I can to help you."

"Thank you. I better head back to Mark's for some clothes and then to work. I am going to ask for a week off so that I can spend time with you and get settled here. Expect some more childish movies," she chirps with a bright smile.

"That sounds perfect. I do not want you to leave, but knowing you will be back makes it more bearable. Even knowing my fate of sitting through children's tales." I lean down and kiss her on her forehead as I pull her into a hug.

I watch as she pulls out of the driveway and out of view. I stand here thinking back on the last day. My Olive is back. She came back to me and will never leave me again if I have anything to do with it. I will let nothing come between us again, even if that means killing again.

The day goes by slowly. I am trying to busy myself with things that may help Olive, like putting her sheets on the bed and clothes in her drawer. Those things do not fill much time, and I find my mind beginning to wander the later in the day it becomes. The same worries she expressed to me last night, I have for her. What if she decides that I am not good enough? Cannot give her what she needs? What if we never find a way to free me, and she moves on? Our situation is a difficult one. Could I really blame her if she tired of having to hide our love? No, Olive is not like that. She is honest and loves me. She would not leave me again.

It is later than I expect when Olive, another car and a moving truck pull up to the house. Mark gets out of the truck, and I immediately bristle. I am glad she has friends and someone took care of her when I could not, but why him? I know this male wants what is mine. I can feel it even though Olive insists he does not.

They have brought friends, and they are unloading Olive's belongings into the house. Apparently, Olive purchased some new living room furniture today. So, they get it all in the house, and Mark begins setting up her television, while her other friends start to unpack the kitchen items. As Mark shows her how to work it, I notice how he places his hand on the small of her back with familiarity, how he looks down at her with wanting. I do not like this at all. She does not seem to notice, but then she looks up at him, and there is something unspoken between them. I really do not like this. Something has happened. I know it. I growl and push Mark back away from her.

"Sorry, man. I didn't mean anything by being so close," Mark says, looking pale, holding his hands in the air, making himself look innocent.

"Seriously, play nice. You didn't have to do that." Olive chastises.

Apparently, I did have to do something. They were clearly making no move to separate. Olive is mine. MINE. I will not have some other male touching her, gazing upon her, wanting and hungry for what belongs to me. Now she is siding with him? She loves me, but allows him to touch her the way I should be? We must speak about this later. This cannot happen.

“Sorry, someone forgets their manners sometimes. Come on, let’s go eat.” Olive says as they walk to the kitchen, where the others are.

I am shocked at the way she is acting. Mark obviously knows about me. Has she not disclosed our relationship? Is she ashamed of me? Thoroughly hurt and becoming more and more angry, I go to our room to get away from the others. I thought things would be different having the house with just Olive and me. Could she be using me for when we are alone and still seeing other human males? I pace the room until she finally comes in after everyone has left.

“I know you're upset, and I am exhausted. Can we go to bed and talk about things? Please?”

I wait a few seconds and then get into the bed without her, silently agreeing but getting my displeasure across. She climbs in beside me, sliding in close. I cannot resist wrapping my arm around her as I drift off.

“I’m sorry I spoke to you that way. It just shocked me when you pushed him.”

“You are mine, Olive. I see how he looks at you, how he touches you. I do not like it. It is more than just friends.”

She draws a deep breath and lets it out. “I know.”

“What do you mean you know?” I am shocked at the admission.

“Don’t freak out. He kissed me and told me he was confused about how he felt about me.” She spits out quickly and then waits for my reaction.

“I will kill him.”

“No, you can’t do that. He is still my friend.”

“He kissed you without your permission, and he is still your friend?” I say angrily.

“It wasn’t without my permission," she admits. I am gutted. I get out of bed and back away from her.

“I’m so sorry. It was at a party, and we had been drinking. I wasn’t thinking clearly, and it just happened. Afterwards, we sat down and agreed that we should just be friends. If I could take it back, I would. Please believe me.”

I say nothing. I stare at her from across the room. Tears are now involuntarily falling down my face. While I was hidden away in the darkness, she was at a party kissing another male. Not thinking of me, not loving me. I cannot do this. I force myself awake and leave her in the bed, sleeping.

Chapter 49: Olive

I can't look him in the eyes. He is so hurt and betrayed by my admission. What have I done? How could I do this to him? He backs away from me, and I don't blame him. I know he will need space and time before he is ready to even look at me again. It was so stupid to kiss Mark. HE is who I want, and now, I may have ruined that. I look up at him, and he is crying. I can't take it and I lower my head again. The next time I look up, he is gone.

I wake up alone, cold in our bed. I can't be here, not without him. I know I should give him space, but I want to fix this. How do I even begin to? I head downstairs, and the feeling of overwhelming sadness hits me like a ton of bricks.

"Please. I am sorry. What can I do to fix this?" My answer is a wave of anger, and then he is gone again. I sink down until I am sitting on the stairs. I lean against the railings, hoping he comes back, hoping I wake up and this is a bad dream. None of this happens and I cry myself to sleep sitting on the stairs.

I wake up to the sunlight creeping up the stairs. My back is aching, but it is nothing compared to the pain I have caused because of what I have done. I have one more day at work before the weekend and then my week off. I go back to our room and get an outfit out of one of the unpacked boxes. I go downstairs to the kitchen to make some coffee. I feel him everywhere. It is a suffocating misery.

I choke back a sob, "I am sorry. Please, let me fix this. Please." I get no answer and I deserve that. I turn around and leave without making the coffee.

Mark knows something is wrong as soon as he sees me. At first, he doesn't pry. As the morning goes on though, he gets concerned over my unusual quiet.

"Olive, what happened after we left last night? Did he hurt you?"

"What? No. He would never hurt me. I hurt him and I don't think he will be able to forgive me."

"The guy literally committed murder for you. I think he will get over whatever it is." he says quietly.

"I told him we kissed on New Year's Eve."

"Olive, that was my fault. I surprised you with that."

"Mark, I was a willing participant. He knew something was up between us. I don't know how, but he did. So, I told him. If I am able to free him, I would not want to start things with secrets you know."

"I get it, Olive, but please be careful. I'm not sure you should free this guy. I don't want you in danger."

"I know he would never hurt me or anyone that didn't really deserve it."

"Olive, I know we said we would leave it just a kiss…" Mark starts.

"We are leaving it at that. You are my best friend. I can't lose that. I promise I'm not in danger."

"You will never lose me, Olive. I am at your side no matter what. I will have to just trust your judgment on this. Just please be careful."

"I will. I promise."

We finish up for the day, and I head to the store to get groceries for my next week off. I take my time shopping. It's not like I need to hurry home. I know he needs space, and when I am there, I just want to seek him out. As I walk through the store, I see other couples and families, all seemingly happy. I hurry through the rest of my shopping and leave the store. My heart can't take seeing others happy when I know I may have just ended my chance at it.

I pull up to the dark house, cursing myself for not leaving a light on in the front of the house. The lights are on in the kitchen, so I walk to the back door to go in that way. As I am going up the steps, I slip, fall, and my face hits the deck. It is a good thing there is a cushion of snow because I would have totally broken my nose. Even though I know it's not broken, it is definitely bleeding. Like a lot. I get into the house as quickly as I can and go to the downstairs bathroom to clean up. As I open the bathroom door, HE rushes to me and grabs my face, turning it from side to side as if he is inspecting it.

“I’m fine. I just fell and landed on my face.” He tucks my hair behind my ear and caresses my face. I lean into his touch and close my eyes.

“I promise I’m ok. I'm a little embarrassed, but physically, I’m good.” I give him a small smile. Satisfied with my answer and what he sees, he slips away once again.

As soon as he is gone, I miss his touch. His absence leaves me cold and feeling so alone. I go to the back deck to gather my things and find that they have already been moved inside. I smile to myself at his thoughtfulness. At least he still cares. It isn’t forgiveness. I know he isn’t there yet. But it's a start. I put all of my groceries away and start to make a quick sandwich for dinner, but I am just not hungry. Instead, I put everything back and leave the kitchen. I feel him watching me, but I say nothing. I don’t want to push him too much. I head up the stairs to shower and change, but he doesn’t follow.

Standing in the shower, I let the hot water wash over me. The tears come quickly, and before I know it, I am weeping uncontrollably for the love I have ruined. He trusted me, and I broke that. I am no better than every other person who has done the very same things to me my whole life. I get a little bit of attention, and I turn into someone I don’t know. This realization hits me hard, and I cry out. The next thing I know, the bathroom door swings open, and the curtain opens. His strong arms are around me as we sink down into the shower together. I lean into him, sobbing and apologizing. He runs his hands through my wet hair, comforting me. I feel him shaking as he is crying himself. We stay in the shower like this for a while until he turns the water off and wraps me in a towel. He pulls me up and leads me to our room. I start to dress, and then he is gone again. I can't stay here without him. So, I grab a blanket and head down to the sofa.

I feel him sit at the other end after I lie down and turn the television on. He doesn't touch me, just sits.

"Thank you for helping me tonight. I know you probably don't want to be near me and totally understand that, but still, thank you for being there." He doesn't make a move for the recorder beside him, but he also doesn't get up. I end up falling asleep watching a show about a recent archaeological dig in Egypt.

When I wake, I see him sitting at the end of the couch with his head in his hands. He must be ready to talk, so he came to our dreamstate. I get up and kneel in front of him, placing my hands on his knees.

"I know my voice is probably the last sound you want to hear. Honestly, I wouldn't blame you. I need to say something because you deserve the truth, not some stupid excuses and a weak version of it." I take a deep breath and continue, "I kissed Mark. I did that. I crossed a line that I swore to you I wouldn't. I broke my promises, and I hurt you. I was selfish and didn't stop and think about you, about us. I did that, and that is on me. I didn't kiss him because it meant something. Because it didn't. It doesn't. That moment was stupid, and I regret it so much. But *you*? You mean everything to me, and that makes this so much worse. You have given me pieces of yourself. You have treated me like I am someone worth loving, worth protecting, and I threw that away. For nothing. I broke the thing I should have protected the most.

I know you can't forgive me now. I'm not asking that. I just want you to know that I am here. I will be here. Owning this. Owning what I have done. I will do whatever it takes to earn your trust back, even if that means waiting outside the walls you have built around yourself. I will never cross another line again. You don't owe me a second chance, but I will be here hoping to be worthy of one someday."

Chapter 50: HIM

I do not look at her right away. I look at the floor, keeping my breaths slow trying not to shatter completely.

"You tell me that he doesn't mean anything, that he is just a friend. Yet you still gave him a part of yourself that was supposed to be mine." I look at her not just with anger, but with betrayal. With loss.

"I cannot help but to keep seeing you with him over and over in my head, Olive. I do not want to torture myself this way, but I cannot turn it off. You can say that it meant- that it means- nothing to you, but it does to me. It means that in that moment, I was not enough. Our love was not enough. Whatever we had…it did not hold you, Olive." I take a breath and close my eyes, trying to refocus all of my anger and hurt. "I do not hate you. It would be easier if I did. I love you, Olive. That is why this hurts so fucking bad. I trusted you. I have never trusted anyone in this life. I gave you my heart and you just…dropped it. It is shattered. When you ask how you can fix this, I do not know. I want to, but I do not know if such a thing is possible." I move closer to her. Closer to the truth. "I hear you apologize. I see your regret. I do not yet know how to let go of this feeling of being replaced even for a second." I pause and look at her in her red, tear filled eyes, "I want to forgive you. Despite everything, I see the girl I fell in love with. I want you, and I do forgive you. I need time and space to get past this. Tonight, I do not know if I can hold this pain and you at the same time."

She lowers her head, crying silently, and it takes all of my resolve not to grab her and pull her in and not let go.

"I understand," she says quietly. She tries to get up and move, and my resolve breaks. I pull her into me and hold her while we both release our hurt and sadness. I let go of her and give her one last look, and then wake up.

Over the next couple of days, she did not push or beg me. When I was feeling angry or sad and needed space, she gave it to me and was there when I came back. I cannot continue like this, though. I miss her. I miss us. She has not been sleeping in our bed, since I have not either. That ends now. She starts to lie down in the living room once again, but I take her hand and stop her. I gently pull her toward our room upstairs. Once there, she gets in the bed and I follow her in, wrapping my arms around her. I feel her warm tears on my chest right before we both start off to sleep.

"At times, I have tried to hate you. At times, I convinced myself that I did. But even in those moments, I would catch myself wondering if you missed me." I said as soon as we woke in our place. She does not interrupt, but her breath catches as she listens. "Holding on to the pain is not making it hurt less. It is just keeping me stuck in one place. You broke something in me, but you also stayed and let me feel what I need to feel to move past this. I see this, Olive. I feel this.

I am still healing, but I love you more than I hate what happened. I want to get over this together. I choose you, my Olive. I choose us." My words hang in the air for moments. She is quiet, as if she cannot quite believe what I am saying. She looks up at me, her eyes full of tears.

"You choose me?", her voice barely a whisper.

"I will always choose you, my Olive."

I push her hair behind her ear, and she leans into my touch, like she is starving for it. I lead her into a kiss, not anything rushed or desperate. Something familiar. Something filled with every unspoken thing we could not say while we were hurting. She sighs and curls her hand into my hair, and I rest my forehead on hers.

"Is this okay?" She asks softly.

"This is everything, Olive."

We do not rush into anything. We hold each other like we are making sure we do not drift apart again. Arms wrapped around each other, legs tangled together. Everything narrows to the sound of our heartbeats in this quiet place. Here we begin again, not where we left off but somewhere new. Stronger.

Chapter 51: Olive

I have made up my mind. I am freeing him, and if I am being honest, it has always been what was going to happen. I think, no, I know, all the doubt was because I am so insecure. I have been researching how to create and use seals. I don't want to create something that is physical and could be found and used against him later. I am wondering if I drew something on him representing a seal for him, if it could work. If it is on him, he would have control over himself, and no one could trap or call on him against his will again. I do not want to tell him just yet because I do not want to let him down if this doesn't work. I know that some things from our dreamstate carry over to the waking world, so hopefully, markings will too.

"What are you thinking, my Olive?"

"About us. Our future."

"I think about that often as well."

"Really? Even now?"

"Yes. I admit I thought there was none for us for a bit, but there is no me without you, Olive. I would cease to be. We were meant to find each other in this life."

"What do you see in our future?"

"I see myself wherever you are. You want to travel to far off places? Then, that is where we go. You want a family and settle here? Then, we are here. It does not matter the location. My future is you. It is us."

"I want everything," I say half jokingly.

"Then I shall make sure you have it all, my Olive."

"I want to make sure you have what you want, too."

"If I have you, then I have everything."

I lean up and kiss him softly, slowly. I want to show him that he is everything to me as well. He puts his hand in my hair and deepens the kiss. As I move my hand lower on his stomach, I start to wake up.

"Ugh! Not now." I grumble into his lips.

"We will have all the time in the world now, Olive. Go ahead and wake up." He says with a low chuckle.

When I wake up, he pulls me close, and I feel him kiss the top of my head. We lie like this for several minutes in the silence of our room, the sun peeking in the windows.

"I'm going to work on hanging curtains and decorating the living room today. Would you like to help me? Maybe watch a movie later?"

"I would like that very much. As for the movie, is it another children's movie?" He says into the recorder.

"No," I say, elbowing him slightly, "How about we watch two? One my pick, and one your pick?"

"This sounds fair. I can live with this."

"It's a date! Come on, let's get started."

We work all morning on hanging blinds, curtains, and some art around the living room, and it is finally feeling like our space. We set up bookshelves and place all my academic books on them for display. I am keeping my spicy books for the bedroom. My stomach begins to protest not being fed around noon, and he insists we stop and make me some lunch.

"I am going to take a shower," I get up and head toward the stairs. "Would you like to join me?" I say in a flirty tone. He rushes by me, and I hear the water turn on in the bathroom before I can even make it up the stairs.

I slip out of my clothes and step into the shower, letting the hot water beat against my shoulders, loosening the tension from the past several days. I tilt my head back, letting the heat seep into every inch of me. Then I feel him get in, and my lips curve into a smile before he even touches me. His hands are slow, like he has all the time in the world. He skims his fingertips along my waist, then lower, dragging the heat from inside me to the surface. He presses against me, and I feel just how much he wants this against my stomach. He kisses me, hungry and possessive. I feel his lips brush against my neck, and it sends a shiver through my body, making my nipples hard. He notices and takes one into his mouth. I moan, my hand finding the back of his head, and I tangle it into his hair. His hands know my body, but today they are relearning it. I close my eyes, and when I open them again, I can see him.

"I can see you, like actually see you," I say, looking into his eyes.

"I have been working on controlling this so I can be with you more," he says, smiling. God, that smile. He leans in and kisses me deeper, pushing me against the cool tile. He lifts my leg up, and I wrap it around him. Our breathing is heavier, and every touch is more intentional. My hand slides up his chest, feeling the heat of his slick skin. His mouth moves to my jaw, my neck, leaving heat with every press of his lips. I gasp softly and pull him closer by threading my fingers in his wet hair. The water fades into the background as he turns me around and bends me forward.

He kisses his way up my spine and whispers in my ear, "You undo me, Olive." With that, he lines up to my entrance and thrusts into me, causing me to gasp at the sudden fullness. He tangles one hand in my hair and pulls my head back slightly, and holds my hip with the other while he rhythmically thrusts into me. His hands hold me possessively like I am his, and he is never letting me go. This isn't just sex; this is something more. He moves inside of me like he has always meant to be there, like this was always meant to happen. With my hands against the tile wall, I moan, and that was all it took to bring him closer to the edge.

“Come for me, Olive,” he says, deep and breathless. I have never heard him speak that way, and it sends me over the edge with him following me.

“I believe I must shower with you more often.” He says as we towel off.

“I believe I would be just fine with that.” I tease, getting on my tip toes for a kiss, which he happily gives me.

***

“It is time for our date, correct?”

“Yep! I have the perfect romance picked out for us,” I say excitedly.

“Wonderful.” I roll my eyes at his obvious sarcasm.

I sit on the couch in my fuzzy socks and an oversized shirt with a warm, fluffy blanket, waiting for *Mister Grumpy* standing in the doorway.

“Quit being so grumpy. You agreed to this.”

“That was earlier, before I actually had to watch it," he says with a smirk.

“Come on, it’s one movie about feelings.”

“Feelings are dangerous, Olive.”

“So are you, Love. Now sit.” He lets out a dramatic sigh and drops into the seat beside me, “Don’t give me that Warrior face. You will love it.”

“No one is even bleeding!” he exclaims, eyeing the screen.

“Exactly. Just kissing and falling in love.”

As the movie plays on, I sneak peeks up at his face from where I am snuggled up to him. He is watching intently. His brow furrows when there is heartbreak. His jaw tightens when the couple fights. When they finally kiss, he looks at me, and I smile at him.

“Do you like it?”

“I like you,” he says softly.

“I’m taking that as a yes.”

“Olive.”

“Yes?”

“It is my turn to torture you,” he laughs. Oh, that sound. It is my favorite sound. Note to self: make him laugh more.

“Do your worst, Warrior!”

“I like this new name. It is strong like me,” he says as he wags his brows. That makes me laugh, and that earns me another one from him.

"Okay, so what am I in for? Something explodes in the first two minutes, doesn't it?"

"Explodes and catches fire."

"I should've known. I show you one soft kiss in the rain, and now I'm watching sweaty men scream in slow motion."

"This is art, Olive. It has a deep plot and lots of feelings and emotion."

"Is this the one where he fights a bear?"

"And wins!" he says proudly, grinning.

I don't complain about the movie and actually get into it, which I think surprises him. I lean into him and gasp at the fights and even cheer at the final battle scene.

"That was really good!"

"I knew you would come around," he says smugly.

"Don't get cocky, Warrior. I'm picking the next movie."

"As long as I get to hold you through it," he says, pulling me into his lap.

"Deal." I seal the promise with a kiss.

Since he is in corporeal form, now would be the perfect time to draw on the seal. I just have to trick him into letting me. I don't want to lie to him, but I want to surprise him and free him.

"My love, I have a question. Would you let me draw you a new tattoo on your side?" On his side would be perfect because it would be hidden.

"Only if I can do one for you."

"Oh, I would love that!" I grab my permanent markers and begin drawing while I explain to him why I chose this design. "I chose the broken arrows and circles because many cultures feel like the broken arrows are a symbol of peace and a desire for harmony. The circles are for wholeness and interconnectedness of all things. Together, they can stand for peace and moving forward from past struggles. I thought these things represent you well. You came from a state of such anger, and now, you just want a peaceful existence. Once you are free, you will be whole and everything will have come full circle for you."

"I like this, Olive. You put a lot of thought into it, and it means everything that you think of me in these ways. When I am free, I will get this on me permanently."

"Your turn, my Olive. Give me your forearm, please." I comply, and he continues, "I read once that feathers symbolize a link between the earthly realm and the spiritual one. Considering our situations, I cannot think of anything more fitting. Of course, I am making this one special for you specifically." I watch him work. He is so gorgeous. How did I get so lucky? He is perfect. I cannot wait to surprise him.

"This is beautiful. Thank you."

"You are welcome, my Olive. I love you."

"I love you more than you will ever know."

He kisses me. "Let's go to bed."

He doesn't have to ask me twice.

I wake up this morning so excited for the day to come. I have decided that I am going to get the feather he drew tattooed on me permanently and then come home and try to free him. I want to make it a whole big event for him. I am going to get candles and light them up everywhere and make it so memorable for us. I let him know I have to run out for a couple of hours, and when I get back, I have a surprise for him. Then I'm out the door to prepare for the night. Finally, everything is coming together for us.

Chapter 52: HIM

She leaves early this morning and says she has a surprise for me this evening. I must admit, I am curious and maybe a little excited. I thought it was different. She wanted to draw on me last night, but I quite enjoyed the activity, and she did an excellent job. It fits me perfectly, and I plan to make it permanent when I am free. That has me thinking. I wonder if she has heard from her contact yet. No, she would have said something. This is too important to hide. Unless that is the surprise. That sure would be one hell of a surprise. Perhaps that is what she is doing today. I try and fail at getting my hopes up.

While she is gone, I can at least help her unpack some boxes that she has not gotten to yet. I head to our bedroom and start working. I work on hanging her clothes in the closet and sorting them into the correct drawers. I move on to her books and thumb through several, noting some things we should try later. I get all of her shelf decorations set out just like she likes them. I get to the last box, which is all her journals and supplies. I am putting her things in her drawers when one of her journals falls open on the floor. I pick it up, not meaning to, and I look down at the page.

I don't know if I can free him now that I know what he is...how can I unleash him into this world?

She knows how to free me? She knows who I am? What I am? I drop the journal to the floor. She has betrayed me again. Every word, every touch, all of it has been poison wrapped in the facade of love. My trust, my soul, everything I gave her is shattered. I want to believe this was a momentary lapse, but why has she not said anything? Has it all been a lie? I am trying to hold on to a small bit of hope that this is a misunderstanding, but I am consumed by such rage that it is becoming increasingly difficult to think clearly.

I look over at the wall and see a framed picture of Mark and her. Is she in love with him? Is this why she does not want to free me? I throw the picture across the room and shatter the frame. I leave our room and go downstairs. What am I to do when she gets home?

As if summoned, I hear her car pull in the drive. I pace the living room, waiting for her to come in. She enters and looks so happy that it catches me off guard.

"I feel you, but can you make yourself where I can see you?" I oblige, and she frowns.

"What's wrong? Are you okay, my love?"

"You said forever. You looked me in the eyes and swore." I say keeping my voice low.

"I meant it. Every word. What is this about?"

"Was it all a lie? Every kiss? Every time we were together?" I raise my voice, and she backs away. "You let me fall for you, let me need you."

"I don't know what you are talking about."

"I saw your journal, OLIVE. How long have you been planning all of this?"

"I…I don't…"

"I was so stupid thinking that you would free me."

"Oh…I think that…"

"SILENCE!" I scream so loud the windows rattle. Her eyes are wide as she backs into the wall. I walk to her and look down at her.

She takes her small hand and reaches out and touches my side where she drew a symbol last night. She looks up at my eyes, full of tears.

"I love you…Malsumis."

Everything happens so fast. I am not myself for several moments as I am filled with raw rage and power. I can see myself, but am unable to stop from grabbing her delicate neck and snapping it.

www.ingramcontent.com/pod-product-compliance
Lightning Source LLC
Chambersburg PA
CBHW071548110726
47908CB00007B/2038

* 9 7 9 8 9 9 3 5 6 8 6 1 4 *